"When can you start?"

Kersty stared at him. "You . . . you mean . . . I've got the job?" Neil nodded. "Don't you want to see some samples of my work?"

"Have you done anything on this scale before?" he demanded.

"Well . . . no," she admitted.

"Then it wouldn't really help, would it?" He stood up suddenly and, pushing his hands into his pockets, strode to the window and stared out.

"But you hardly know me," Kersty blurted. "Aren't you taking a terrible risk?"

Neil turned. He gazed at her long and hard, his expression deeply thoughtful. "Hardly know you? I wouldn't say that, Kersty. I wouldn't say that at all."

Dana James lives with her husband and three children in a converted barn on the edge of a Cornish village. She has written thrillers, historical romances and doctor-nurse romances but is now concentrating her efforts on writing comtemporary romance fiction. In addition to extensive researching, which she adores, the author tries to write for a least four hours every day.

Pool of Dreaming
Dana James

Harlequin Books

TORONTO • NEW YORK • LONDON
AMSTERDAM • PARIS • SYDNEY • HAMBURG
STOCKHOLM • ATHENS • TOKYO • MILAN

Original hardcover edition published in 1988
by Mills & Boon Limited

ISBN 0-373-02992-6

Harlequin Romance first edition July 1989

For their generous assistance
I wish to extend my grateful thanks to:

Della, Kathy and Clare at Delta Graphics
and
Peter Scott of Firefox Marketing

CHAPTER ONE

'DAMN!' Kersty muttered with quiet force, and hollowed her back to ease free of the barbed wire. It had pierced her sweater and shirt, and she could feel the rusty metal point digging into the skin below her shoulder-blade. She twisted and squirmed, but it was impossible. The barb only gouged deeper into her flesh. And it hurt.

Flicking her long hair back, in an attempt to see which way the barbs were pointing, she winced as a wind-blown curl caught on the wire and was held fast.

This was too ridiculous. She had got through the first fence on the edge of the wood quite easily, despite the strong new posts and shiny wire with vicious, claw-like hooks.

She had been no less careful here, where the wood met rolling parkland dotted with magnificent copper beeches and huge oaks. So how on earth had she managed to get caught up on these older, looser strands?

Bent forward from the waist, her blue-jeaned legs astride the lower twist of wire, both hands occupied in trying to keep the wires apart, she was well and truly a prisoner.

The rustle of approaching footsteps brought Kersty's head up with a jerk. She smothered a cry of pain. She'd forgotten her hair was caught, and her reflex movement had forced the barb deeper into her flesh.

The leisurely stride came nearer and Kersty's heartbeat quickened. Should she call for help, or keep quiet and hope that he, for she sensed it was a man, would pass by without seeing her?

She was screened from both the woods and the over-grown path bordering the park by thick bushes.

But if she didn't ask for help, how was she going to get free? The more she struggled, the deeper the barb would work its way in.

She looked down at the wire between her knees. As well as flaking rust, it was adorned with bits of mouldy leaf, fluff—perhaps from a rabbit—and bird-lime. A dose of blood-poisoning on top of everything else really would be the last straw.

Kersty swallowed hard. What if he was a poacher? It was May, she reminded herself quickly. There was nothing to poach other than rabbits or pigeons. Even so, he might not be exactly pleased at someone seeing him where he had no business to be. But she had no right to be there, either, so that made them equal.

'I—I say,' she shouted. The footsteps stopped. 'Can you help me, please? I'm caught on the wire.'

There was a moment's silence. Kersty wondered if she should shout again. Then a twig snapped and the footsteps drew nearer. To the right of Kersty's head the bushes rustled and parted.

The man who stood there was at least six feet tall, and from Kersty's angle of vision seemed almost twice that. She gulped. Faded blue jeans hugging narrow hips and firmly muscled thighs were tucked into mud-spattered green Hunter boots. The rolled-up sleeves and open neck of a pale blue denim shirt revealed mahogany skin and dark, curling hair. Broad shoulders and a strong neck supported a hard-planed face shadowed by faint beard stubble. Narrowed eyes observed her from beneath straight brows, and sunstreaked hair, tousled by the breeze, fell across his forehead.

He took another step forward and Kersty saw, bal-anced on his shoulder, his finger hooked round the trigger guard, a double-barrelled shotgun.

'Look, I promise I won't tell anyone,' she blurted breathlessly. 'If you'll just unhook me, no one need know either of us has been here.'

At the look of mild puzzlement on the man's face, Kersty's heart sank. 'You're not a poacher.'

His wide mouth tightened for an instant in a fleeting expression which could have registered anger or amusement. He shook his head slowly.

Kersty sighed. 'I suppose you work on the estate.' She was so concerned with the implications of being caught in such damning circumstances, she did not notice the momentary hesitation before he nodded.

'Yes,' he said briefly. 'Are you local?' His voice was deep and smooth and made Kersty think of dark, flowing honey.

Of all the things to be imagining at a time like this! She was glad her hair screened the pinkness in her cheeks. 'I live in the village, yes,' she admitted.

'May I ask what brings you to Ravenswood?' His courtesy only emphasised the undertone of amusement.

'Do you think you might unhook me first?' Kersty demanded with acid sweetness. 'I find that being strung up on barbed wire rather inhibits my facility for polite conversation.'

'Really,' the stranger mused, 'I would have thought it quite…persuasive.' He remained exactly where he was, weight on his left foot, left hand in the front pocket of his jeans, the gun resting casually on his right shoulder.

Panic fluttered in Kersty. 'I will explain, I promise,' she said quickly. 'Only, please, help me get free. One of the barbs is sticking in my back and——'

In one swift movement he had set the gun down and come to her side. Sunlight glinted on the barrel, and Kersty was startled to see the name James Purdey engraved in flowing script on the metal. She had designed a catalogue for an antique dealer about a year ago, and he had been offering a pair of Purdeys for sale. She could not remember the exact valuation, but it had been several thousand pounds. Why would an estate worker be carrying such a valuable firearm?

Kersty's brief curiosity dissolved as her gaze shifted and she caught sight of the two cartridges in the breech. An icy shiver rippled down her spine. Don't be stupid, she told herself. People don't get *shot* for trespassing. Not these days, not in this country.

He freed her hair first, and she groaned with relief, dropping her head forward and turning it from side to side to ease the stiffness in her neck and shoulders. His booted foot on the lower wire enabled her to release her grip and she flexed her fingers.

'Stand quite still,' he commanded softly, and Kersty bit back a gasp as he carefully removed the barb. From the sting and sudden warmth she knew the wound was more than a mere graze.

Grabbing his hand to stop herself overbalancing, she stepped through the parted wires towards him.

Free at last, she began to straighten up, but before she could utter a word, he spun her round so her back was towards him, placed her palms against the nearest tree and, pushing up her sweater, pulled her shirt free from the waistband of her jeans.

Leaping like a scalded cat, Kersty whirled round. 'What the hell do you think you're doing?' she blazed, backing away from him.

Once again his mouth quirked fleetingly. 'Trying to minimise the risk of infection,' came the calm reply. 'What on earth did you imagine? If the wound is bleeding freely it will take only a few seconds. When did you have your last tetanus shot?'

Before she realised what was happening, he had gently replaced her hands against the tree. As she recalled her earlier fears of blood-poisoning, it wasn't only the sudden awareness of the cool air against her bare back that made her shiver. 'I—I'm not sure, last year I think.

Look, wait——' she cried desperately, craning her head over her shoulder, 'I don't even know your name.'

'I doubt that will affect the treatment,' he said drily, 'but it's Neil, Neil Drummond. Now turn your head around and please try to keep still.'

Kersty did as she was told. Her eyes widened with shock and every muscle tensed as Neil Drummond's mouth fastened over the wound. He sucked hard for several seconds then, lifting his head, turned away and spat. After repeating the process twice more, he straightened up.

'Your shirt's in a mess, but it's nothing cold water and salt won't cure,' he observed.

Kersty felt no pain, just a throbbing warmth.

'I don't suppose you carry sticking plaster or antiseptic cream?' It was a rhetorical question and he answered it himself. 'I thought not. Don't move,' he ordered as she tried to stand up straight. He raked in his own pockets and produced a pristine white handkerchief, still neatly folded. Shaking it out, and using her lower back, he folded it into four. 'People who risk life and limb trespassing on property which is fenced off for their own safety——' He broke off and, lifting the shoulder strap of her bra over the side of the improvised pad to hold it in place, he tucked the lower edge beneath the fastening band. His fingers were warm and quite impersonal. He did not linger, nor did he touch her more than was necessary as he lifted her shirt down carefully over the dressing. 'Such people ought at least to come prepared for accidents.' He stood back. 'You can tuck yourself in.'

Kersty shot upright, her face on fire, her skin tingling from the memory of his touch, and her fingers all thumbs as she stuffed her shirt back into the waistband of her jeans. 'I've lived in the village most of my life,' she retorted, 'and *I* never heard of anyone coming to harm on the estate. The Carvossas never used to mind people walking through the woods. The new owner must be paranoid.' Kersty didn't hide her disgust. 'This place is almost as well protected as Fort Knox.'

'It is *private* property.' He did not raise his voice, but a new element had crept in, a steeliness that raised goosepimples on Kersty's heated skin. 'Apart from the fact that we are clearing areas of the wood, which involves the use of chainsaws, JCBs and heavy lorries, all dangerous to the unwary, there are no public rights of way on the deeds. If the local people were allowed access in the past, it was due solely to the goodwill of the owner, not as a legal right.'

'You seem to know a lot about it,' she observed tartly, stung by the rebuke and forced by her innate honesty to admit it was deserved.

He smiled down at her, and it was as if a newer, brighter sun had appeared in the sky. The smile lit up his face, making him look suddenly years younger and somehow much more approachable. His eyes, a deep, cornflower blue, were startling in his darkly weathered face, and danced with amusement. Yet there was something in their depths which, while not exactly making her uneasy, confused Kersty.

He shrugged lightly. 'All part of the job. Would you care for some tea?'

Caught off balance by the unexpected offer, she hesitated. 'Oh, I—I don't think——'

He cut in smoothly. 'You promised, if I freed you, to tell me why you were sneaking about in here.' He leaned over and scooped up the gun, balancing it on his shoulder once more. There was nothing *overtly* threatening about the movement, and yet...

'I was not sneaking,' Kersty protested hotly. 'I was walking perfectly normally.'

'Not when you called for help,' he reminded her. His mouth twitched briefly. 'Shall we go?' Parting the bushes with one hand, he stood back to let her pass, and for no apparent reason she suddenly found herself reliving the sensation of his mouth on her skin, the scrape of his beard, and the firm warmth of his hands. There was a strange quivering beneath her ribs, and Kersty lowered her head, letting her hair swing forward as she passed him. 'Th-thank you,' she muttered.

'It was my pleasure.' The undercurrent of amusement warmed her cheeks, and she had the oddest feeling that he had guessed her thoughts.

Last year's leaves whispered beneath their feet as they reached a fork in the deeply rutted path and headed in the general direction of the lake.

'I—I used to know these woods like the back of my hand,' Kersty found herself saying as the silence grew unbearable. 'I'd no idea the estate had become so badly run down.'

He glanced at her, polite, interested. 'You haven't been in here for a while, then?'

She caught his eye, but could detect no sarcasm or hidden meaning in the question. Shaking her head, she answered truthfully, 'Not for years. But when I was a child, it was a magical place. Trees blown down by winter gales often blocked the paths. Sometimes they'd be sawn up and cleared away, but more often they were just left to rot.' She glanced at him from beneath long eyelashes. 'Poor estate management, but terrific fun. We climbed on them and hid behind them. They were horses to ride, ships at sea, and islands in crocodile-infested swamps.

'In the spring, we used to go to the lake to collect frogspawn and pick bluebells. On hot summer days, we'd bring a picnic and sit in the grass where the park meets the woods, and listen to the birds. We'd see how many different butterflies we could count and watch the squirrels. Then in autumn there were blackberries to pick, and conkers.' She darted another look at him, grinning guiltily. 'If we were feeling very brave, we'd go scrumping apples from the orchard, too. Then, when winter came, we'd put on scarves, wellies and thick gloves and collect chestnuts.' Kersty smiled at the memory. 'It was like discovering treasure to split open the prickly cases and see the nuts, all fat and glossy, packed tight inside.'

She gazed about her at the deeply rutted earth, scarred by the passage of heavy vehicles, the piles of sawdust, the pyramids of stacked logs with numbers painted on their freshly sawn trunks. 'It all looks so different now.'

'You are no longer a child,' Neil pointed out.

'No,' she agreed softly. Hopelessness welled up inside her. There was no escape from the present and all its pressures, problems and decisions. *Decisions.* Kersty shivered, suddenly cold.

'I don't think I caught your name,' Neil said.

Kersty dragged her attention back to him, obscurely angry. 'I didn't give it,' she replied shortly. She was behaving badly. The knowledge made her even more angry, but now the anger was directed at herself. It wasn't his fault. She had no right to be rude, especially as, if it hadn't been for him, she would still be impaled on the barbed wire.

'But you're going to,' Neil smiled pleasantly. Behind this calm statement of fact, Kersty glimpsed a determination bordering on ruthlessness. But the impression was only momentary, and his next words drove it from her mind. 'We can hardly chat like old friends over a cup of tea if I don't even know your name.'

Kersty wasn't at all sure she wanted to be friends with Neil Drummond. There was no denying his good looks, and he possessed a quiet charm that made Miles's silver-tongued eloquence seem cloying and studied. But there was something about him, an indefinable air, that seemed at odds with his position as woodsman or estate manager or whatever the correct term was. It wasn't that he was loud-mouthed or over-familiar. In fact, his quiet courtesy had surprised her.

'Your name,' he prompted.

'Kersty.' She spelled it for him. 'Kersty Hurrell.'

'So, Kersty.' His voice was quiet, and its very mildness was a forewarning to her, even as she ridiculed herself for being so fanciful. 'What could be worrying you so much that you try to find escape and comfort in a childhood playground?'

Kersty's head flew up, and before she could stop herself she blurted, 'How did you know?'

He shrugged easily. A grin played at the corners of his mouth. 'I suppose it has to be a man.'

For a moment Kersty didn't know what to say. Nothing about this afternoon had turned out as she had imagined. All right, he'd made a lucky guess. She *had* come back to Ravenswood to recapture the carefree happiness and security of her childhood. And to find the strength to face decisions she knew had to be made. The situation could not be allowed to drift any longer. She had spent too long hoping, praying, that somehow, something would turn up.

She pushed a hand through her hair in a gesture that betrayed her despair. 'You're right,' she admitted. 'Well, partly. But it's not a man in the usual sense.'

He raised one straight brow in silent query.

The path joined a wide, cobbled drive. A few yards further on, a metal fence bisected by a large white-painted gate divided the woods from more parkland rising gently towards massed ranks of tall rhododendron bushes, ablaze with pink, white and purple flowers, bordering the formal gardens which surrounded the house. But, though the blossom-laden bushes were a magnificent sight, it was the sea of bluebells stretching as far as the eye could see that made Kersty catch her breath. The breeze rippled them like water, and the sun gleamed on the fresh new leaves of the tall beech trees, some emerald-green, others glowing copper.

'Oh, it's so beautiful,' Kersty murmured. 'Even more than I remember.'

'Good,' he said softly, and smiled.

Suddenly, Kersty wanted to tell him everything. He was a stranger, so it couldn't mean anything to him. But talking it out might help her come to the right decision. She had kept it all bottled up for so long, having to put on a brave face for Josh, and her father, and the clients. She hadn't even dared confide in Harry, not this time. One word to his sister, Stella, and it would be all over the town in no time. There would be some sympathy, but that was small comfort. The fact that she had failed after being so *sure* of success was a bitter pill to swallow.

She clasped her hands behind her, then stuck them in her pockets as Neil closed the gate behind them and they started up the drive.

'I'm a graphic designer,' she began hesitantly. 'I run my own small business from a studio and office in town.'

'What's your angle?' Neil broke in curiously.

'I—I beg your pardon?'

'Your sales pitch. High quality or low prices?'

'Oh.' Her bewilderment cleared. 'High quality.' He nodded, as though she had confirmed something for him, and she went on, 'But it's a very competitive business, and becoming more so. I've got two clients whose work we need, but they are very slow to pay.' She spread her hands in a gesture of helplessness. 'I'm facing what is commonly known as a cash-flow problem.' She tried to grin, but it wasn't a success. 'Problem? Who am I kidding? It's more of a crisis! The bank won't lend me any more money until I clear some of the overdraft. The fact that I've got a pile of enquiries on my desk for work I'd give my back teeth to do doesn't cut any ice with them at all.' She sighed and jerked her head, flicking her hair back over her shoulder. 'I've also started receiving complaints about late delivery of work. I could soon solve that by taking on more staff, but I simply can't afford to.' She grimaced. 'This is where Miles comes in.'

'Do I take it Miles is the other half of the problem?' Neil queried.

Kersty nodded, pulling a face. 'Oh, he's a real charmer, is Miles. So reasonable, so logical and, though it kills me to admit it, *so right*. It does make economic sense to sell out to him and let K. Graphics become part of the Duchy Design Company. I've been promised a seat on the board, just like the owners of the other two small companies he's swallowed up. He would take on the overdraft as well as the new orders and all my troubles would be over.' She shrugged and flashed a brittle smile at Neil.

'But?' he said softly.

Kersty looked down at her feet, her burnished hair falling forward to mask a face suddenly tight and pinched with misery. 'But it wouldn't be *mine* any more. Without boasting, I'm quite certain Miles Quintrell wouldn't be the least bit interested in buying me out if I didn't present some sort of threat. After all, a little competition is always good for any business. But once he takes over, the individual touch that made K. Graphics something special will be lost. Miles is a great one for levelling down. In any case, the atmosphere could never be the same. And yet,' she raised worried eyes to his, 'do I have the right to deny my staff the security this ... *merger*——' she grimaced '—Miles's diplomatic description—would provide?'

They left the avenue of sycamores and poplars bordering the top of the drive, and turned along a shady path towards a small, stone-built cottage nestling among the trees and surrounded by lawn.

'How many staff are involved?' Neil asked.

Kersty looked up at him with a quick, half-embarrassed smile. 'Perhaps staff isn't quite the right term. It's more of a family affair really, and there are only four of us. Josh, my brother, he's our photographer. And he's brilliant, really talented. Sue, his fiancée, helps me. She does routine jobs in the studio, answers the telephone, types letters, that sort of thing. And there's Harry. He isn't a relation, though he often behaves like a Dutch uncle. He was an artificer in the Royal Navy until he retired. He works miracles keeping our dubbing and editing equipment going. But sooner or later something vital will go bang and even Harry's expertise and boxes of bits won't be enough to fix it.' She heaved a sigh. 'So it comes back to money again.'

Kicking off his mud-crusted boots, Neil unlocked the front door and went in, automatically ducking his head to avoid the low lintel. 'What has dubbing and editing to do with graphic design?' he asked over his shoulder, clearly expecting her to follow him.

Kersty hesitated only a moment. Then, carefully wiping her shoes on the spotless mat, she stepped over the threshold. 'Nothing,' she replied. 'But we also make promotional videos. It's a fast-growing market.' She closed the door. 'All sorts of people are having them done: estate agents, large companies, and the Tourist Boards. But they do cost quite a lot to make, and it's pointless producing a beautifully photographed film if the sound quality of the commentary and background music spoils the presentation.' Her voice trailed off as she looked around, her eyes widening.

The cottage had looked quite small from outside, but Neil had obviously demolished the inner dividing walls, for the room in which Kersty now stood covered the whole of the ground floor.

One window looked out on to the front lawn, while sunlight streamed in through three others which faced south-west. A beamed ceiling, high enough for Neil to stand upright with inches to spare, honey-coloured walls, and, at the far end, an inglenook fireplace with a massive oak lintel gave the room a cosy intimacy heightened by the fire glowing beneath a beaten copper hood. A large basket of logs stood on the stone hearth.

A tall, exotic pot-plant with masses of glossy leaves filled an alcove. Several more plants, with brilliant blooms lifted to the sun, sat on the broad window-sills.

A plain fawn carpet bore the neat stripes of recent vacuuming, and there wasn't a speck of dust to be seen. Warning bells began ringing in Kersty's head. Unmistakably, what little she had seen of the cottage was stamped with a woman's touch. Only a carelessly folded newspaper tossed on to the faded but spotless chintz-covered sofa, and books piled untidily on every available surface, saved the room from the sterile good taste of an advertisement in *Ideal Home*.

Neil reappeared in the doorway opposite, no longer carrying the gun. Beyond him, Kersty glimpsed the streamlined units of a modern kitchen. She thought of the bungalow she shared with her father and Josh, built in the 1930s and hardly altered since, except for redecorating.

'You did say tea?'

'Oh!' Kersty started. 'Y-yes. Thank you.' She hadn't meant to say that. She should have refused, politely, of course. She ought not to be here. It was time to make some excuse and leave.

'Aaaah,' he frowned. 'There is a small, but significant problem. I've run out.'

There it was. He'd offered her the solution. 'It really doesn't matter,' Kersty said quickly, backing away towards the door. 'I'd better be getting home now anyway.'

'I'm sure I put it on yesterday's list for Mrs Laity,' he said, as though she hadn't spoken. 'My housekeeper,' he added. 'Though perhaps the term is a little pretentious.' The corners of his mouth lifted in self-mockery. 'She only comes here once a week. But as I live alone and am reasonably tidy, it doesn't get in too bad a state.'

The glint of amusement in his hooded eyes brought faint colour to Kersty's cheeks. He had recognised her sudden awareness and reserve. The fact that he had bothered to clarify the situation sent an unexpected tingle of pleasure and excitement along her spine.

Then, as she realised the direction her galloping thoughts were taking, Kersty's face began to burn. She had only just met him, and in circumstances that were embarrassing, to say the least.

Besides, after Martin, and with all she had on her plate regarding the business, she certainly wasn't looking for more heartache.

'So, could you bear coffee instead?' Neil queried. 'It's Brazilian special blend. I developed a taste for it while I was working there. One had little choice. It was almost impossible to get anything else.'

'Please don't go to any trouble.'

'Believe me, it's no trouble at all.' His voice, his direct gaze, the warmth of his quick smile, made Kersty falter. Her interest was caught, even though she suspected the casually dropped remark about Brazil was a deft ploy to change the subject and coax her into staying a while longer.

Well, why not? He seemed very pleasant. He certainly had beautiful manners. And it was a long time since she had talked to anyone about matters other than work. Yet work had even crept into this afternoon, although that had been his doing, insisting she tell him why she had come to Ravenswood.

'Have you ever been to South America?' Neil called from the kitchen. He had interpreted her hesitation as acquiescence and was busy with the percolator. 'Do please sit down and make yourself at home.'

At home, not *comfortable*. Kersty gave herself a mental shake. 'Thank you.' She settled herself on the sofa, raising her voice so it would carry over the bubbling of the percolator and the subdued clatter of crockery. 'As a matter of fact,' she confided, 'I've only been out of Cornwall a few times.'

Neil emerged from the kitchen carrying a tray. 'Who could blame you? I've seen quite a bit of the world, and there are few places more beautiful. It has an atmosphere all its own.' He indicated a small table piled high with *National Geographic* and nature magazines. 'Would you mind pushing that lot on to the floor? The table is very light; if you could just lift it over here, we'll be more comfortable by the fire.'

Kersty did as he asked, conscious that, while treating her with a courtesy she had rarely experienced, he was also behaving as though they had known one another for some time. The combination was very seductive, and she found it strangely difficult to maintain her usual reserve and distance.

Dealing with men on a professional basis posed no problems for Kersty. She knew she was good at her job, and discussions were friendly but businesslike. The boundaries were clear, and anyone overstepping them met with a decidedly frosty response. Her head accepted that all men were not like Martin, but her heart recoiled from the risk.

The tray held a beautiful and obviously expensive coffee-pot, cups and saucers, a matching cream-jug and sugar-bowl, and a plate of cherry buns.

Neil caught her eye and grinned. 'No, I didn't,' he said, forestalling her question.

'My,' Kersty observed, tongue firmly in her cheek, 'doesn't Mrs Laity take her work seriously!'

Neil shrugged. 'What can I do with a woman who is convinced I need looking after?'

'Humour her,' Kersty retorted sweetly.

Neil's face registered momentary surprise as her irony hit home, then eyes bright with devilment, he set the tray down in front of her. 'If you would care to pour— by the way, I take mine black with one spoonful of sugar—I'll stir the fire up a bit. In spite of the sunshine, the wind has a keen edge today.'

'Touché,' Kersty muttered under her breath, masking a smile. For all his olde-worlde courtesy, Neil Drummond had a mind like a scalpel. In fact, considering his talent for organising people, she was surprised he had chosen this type of work, hard physical labour, out in all weathers. Surely he could have done better for himself? Of course, it was none of her business. Doubtless he had his own very good reasons. Yet, there was something, she couldn't put her finger on it, but she sensed there was far more to Neil Drummond that he had so far revealed.

CHAPTER TWO

SETTLING herself in the corner of the sofa cradling her coffee-cup, Kersty was acutely aware of Neil beside her. This awareness, so unexpected, so confusing, unnerved her. She racked her brain for something to say. Anything to break the silence which was becoming too cosy and intimate for her peace of mind.

'Was it business or pleasure, your trip to Brazil?' She tried hard to sound merely polite. But, now the question was out, she was startled by her own curiosity.

His mouth curved briefly as he glanced at her. 'It was a little more than a *trip*. I was out there for five years on my——' he corrected himself smoothly '—on a large estate in one of the *terra firma* forests along the Amazon.'

'What's a *terra firma* forest?' Kersty asked, barely noticing the brief hesitation.

'An area above the highest flood levels. The drier ground supports the highest trees. We had timber growing to over a hundred and fifty feet.'

'Was it the same sort of job you're doing here?' She had given up trying to hide her interest.

Neil leaned forward to refill his cup. 'Bits of it were,' he answered carefully. She shook her head as he offered her more coffee. 'I have a degree in forestry, and part of that particular job involved conservation and a re-planting programme, as well as felling mahogany and rosewood for export. But neither the local labour we recruited, nor the relevant government departments, were interested. In their view, replanting was a waste of time and money. There were thousands of square miles of trees, so why worry? All around our estate huge tracts

23

of forest were being cut down. It looked like a battle-
ground: nothing but stumps, sawdust and torn earth.'
His expression had grown hard and Kersty felt a chill
feather across the back of her neck at the quiet, bitter
anger emanating from him. An anger all the more potent
for being controlled. It occurred to her that she would
not care to be on the receiving end of Neil Drummond's
wrath.

'Is—is that why you left and came back to this
country?' No wonder he looked so hard and fit. Demanding physical work in those temperatures and humidity either made or broke a man. Neil Drummond
had not merely survived. He made Kersty think of iron
that had been through a furnace, emerging as tempered
steel.

He shook his head. 'Not entirely. I—there was a death
in the family.' His arm brushed her knee as he replaced
his cup on the tray. It was totally accidental, but the
brief contact sent a buzz along Kersty's taut nerves.

Swallowing, praying he hadn't noticed her quick intake
of breath, she waited for him to go on with what he was
saying. Instead, he changed the subject entirely.

'You must have known the Carvossa family well,
having lived here all your life,' he observed casually.

She shook her head. 'We all knew them by sight, but
they weren't the sort of people you could know *well*.'

'The gentry and the rabble, you mean?' he asked with
feigned innocence.

'No, I do not mean,' she retorted, smiling but meaning
every word. 'You may not have been here long enough
to realise it, but the Cornish are a very independent
people. We give credit where it's due, and respect if it's
earned. But being an island within an island has given
us an... individuality you're unlikely to find elsewhere.'

'I had noticed,' he murmured ironically. 'About the
Carvossas?'

'I only remember Richard and Evangeline,' Kersty replied. 'The rest of the family had died long before I was born.' She put her own cup down. 'The first time I saw Evangeline, she was dressed in a long, flowing gown of pink and green. She had a lilac silk scarf around her neck and was pruning roses. Her hair was as bright as newly minted copper. Mother thought she put henna on it. She always wore lovely vivid colours. I think she must have been over sixty then.'

'An eccentric, would you say?' Neil ventured.

'Actually,' Kersty confided, 'she was as nutty as a fruit cake. But she was harmless. So was her brother Richard. She liked to paint and write poetry and grow roses. He just couldn't cope with the twentieth century. He was a sweet, gentle soul, but he belonged to a different age. It's not really surprising the estate became so run-down and neglected,' she mused. 'When the older staff who understood their odd ways left or died, they couldn't find replacements. At least, not ones who would stay.

'Neither Richard nor Evangeline had a clue about money. It often took a solicitor's letter or threats of court action to get them to pay a bill. They weren't deliberately mean or dishonest,' she added quickly, wanting him to understand. 'It was just that to them money was an irrelevance. As long as there was food in the house and coal for a fire, they weren't interested in how it got there. It simply didn't occur to them that the local shopkeepers and tradesmen had their own bills to pay. Eventually, they just couldn't cope on their own any more, and they both went into a home.'

'You are remarkably well informed.' Neil's dark brows lifted, and Kersty thought she detected the faintest note of censure.

'My mother nursed Evangeline when she fell off a horse and broke her hip. I went with her to help a few times. Evangeline was over seventy then, and still talked of balls they used to have when she was young, and the beaux who wanted to marry her. She never did marry. I often wondered why. Lord, that was... fifteen years ago.' Kersty paused, looking inward to a distant past. 'They're all dead now,' she said softly.

'All?' Neil queried.

Kersty's head lifted. 'Richard, Evangeline... and my mother,' she added, barely realising she spoke aloud.

'Your mother?' Neil frowned. 'Forgive me, but she couldn't have been very old.'

'She wasn't,' Kersty's voice was flat.

'An accident?'

'Cancer.' It was curt, abrupt. Kersty's face tightened. It was not a time she wanted to remember. As well as losing her mother, she had lost her fiancé. Though *lost* was perhaps not the right word. Without telling her, Martin had given up his flat, changed his job and walked out of her life, leaving her with a half-planned wedding, a chest full of things for her new home, and a letter.

Worried sick about her mother, and feeling the strain regarding her newly launched business, she hadn't even realised anything was wrong until she'd opened the envelope and read the brief note inside.

In it he told her he was tired of coming a poor third in her affections after her family and her business, tired of practically having to make an appointment to see her. And that in any case she was not exactly passionate when they were together. He wished her well, but advised her not to consider marrying anyone until she had grown out of her selfishness.

She had laughed then, even as scalding tears had flooded down her cheeks. She had seen him clearly for what he was. But knowing she was better off without him had not lessened the pain of loss, or the brutality of his actions.

She had managed to keep it from her mother, who was too ill to cope with any further upset. Her father had been sympathetic, but most of his concern was for his wife, and Josh had still been at college. With no one in whom she could confide, Kersty had simply thrust it all to the back of her mind. There had been plenty to keep her busy.

After her mother died, slipping away peacefully in her sleep, Kersty had totally immersed herself in her work, finding comfort and escape in building her business. For the past two years she had thought of little else. But now, that too was threatened.

'Forgive me,' Neil's dark, gentle voice broke into her thoughts. 'I have made you unhappy. That was the very last thing I intended.'

Kersty shook her head. 'It's all right, honestly. I just——' She put on a bright smile and deliberately changed the subject. There was something about him that invited confidences, and it would be all too easy to let the hurt flood out. She resisted the temptation. He was pleasant, but he was a man. A man she barely knew, and she had the uneasy feeling she had already told him far more about herself than was wise. 'Who owns Ravenswood now? Did it stay in the family? There have been all sorts of rumours in the village.' Her grin was more natural, less strained. 'But that's nothing new.'

Neil bent forward to toss another log on to the fire. 'What sort of rumours?'

'Oh, you know,' Kersty shrugged. 'It's been bought by a pop star, it's going to be turned into a commune, the land is being sold off for development, the usual sort of thing.'

He nodded, his back towards her. 'Well, they're all wrong. It has remained in the family, though it's a distant branch.' He settled beside her once more, resting one arm casually along the back of the sofa, one leg tucked beneath him.

'Apparently, James Carvossa married twice. Richard and Evangeline were the children of the first marriage. James's second wife was much younger than him and bore him two daughters. One died young, the other married a Scottish peer and produced two daughters and a son. It's the son, Viscount Haldane, who now owns Ravenswood.'

Kersty's brows climbed. 'Now who is well informed?' she commented, only half joking.

Neil seemed momentarily taken aback, then, with an offhand gesture, said, 'I keep my eyes and ears open.'

'Well,' Kersty frowned, 'I can't help thinking it's all wrong that one person should own so much when there are thousands of people in this country who are literally homeless.'

'I take your point,' Neil nodded. 'But even if an estate like Ravenswood could be built on, it wouldn't solve the problem. Most of those people live in cities and have done so all their lives. And in any case, Cornwall is a high unemployment area. Say your suggestion was carried out, where would they find jobs? What would be left of Britain's heritage? Where would people go to escape the concrete jungle of city life? Where then could they enjoy parks, woods and lakes?'

Kersty snorted. 'As Ravenswood has been fenced off with barbed wire for the past two or three years, there has hardly been much opportunity for pleasant walks, or visits to the lake here, for anyone.'

'That situation is not necessarily permanent.'

Kersty's face brightened. 'Does the Viscount intend to reopen it to the public?'

Neil shook his head. 'Not exactly. The plan is to turn the house into a luxury hotel with an indoor pool, jacuzzi, solarium and gym for people who want peace and privacy, and the opportunity to relax and recuperate away from the public eye.'

Kersty looked at him. 'You make it sound like a sort of upmarket health farm.'

He laughed. 'Do I? Well, what better place for it? We're only a mile from the coast, in beautiful surroundings, with fresh eggs, meat and vegetables from the home farms. Don't you approve?'

She sensed he was teasing her, and grinned. 'I'm not a complete Puritan. I'd give my back teeth to be pampered in a place like that. The only reason I've never been to one is that I can't afford it. Still,' she sighed, 'that's not likely to be a problem for Viscount Haldane.'

'What isn't?' Neil seemed confused.

'Money.'

'On the contrary,' Neil's mouth twisted. 'I think he finds it an enormous headache.'

'Come on,' Kersty scoffed. 'He owns an estate like Ravenswood and he's pleading poverty? I should be so poor.'

Neil stood up suddenly, a swift, sinuous movement, and moved to the fireplace. Resting one foot on the hearth, he leaned his shoulder against the stonework, thrusting his hands into his pockets. 'It's not quite that simple.' His voice was taut, controlled. 'The estate is entailed, which means he can't sell it. It has to be passed on to his heirs. So, in effect, he doesn't own it, he merely holds it in trust. When he inherited Ravenswood, he also became liable for a horrendous sum in death duties.'

Kersty looked shaken. 'Goodness, I had no idea.'

'Why should you?' Neil smiled. 'You have problems of your own. But perhaps you can see now why Ravenswood must become a viable commercial enterprise, a business that pays its way.'

Kersty nodded. She sighed again. 'Me, too,' she grinned up at him. 'What I need is a big fat contract, with half the money paid in advance, for a complete advertising package, video and brochures. Then I would tell Miles Quintrell just what he could do with his *merger*.' She was thoughtful for a moment, an idea forming. She turned impulsively to Neil, but before she could speak, the telephone on a side-table chirped softly.

Swinging round, Neil picked up the receiver and listened. 'I'll be with you in a few minutes,' he said, and replaced the receiver.

Kersty was already on her feet. Her shoulder felt a bit stiff and the pad stuck to her skin and she moved gingerly. 'Thank you for the coffee, it was delicious.'

He extended his hand, a curiously formal gesture. But instead of shaking hers, he simply held it, covering it with both of his, and Kersty felt a pulse beating rapidly in her throat. They were standing quite close and he seemed very tall. 'I've enjoyed our conversation enormously.' The rich timbre of his voice slid down her spine and brought goose-pimples up on her arms. 'I'm sure something will work out for you.'

'Yes. Well——' Kersty drew her hand free with an odd reluctance. It had felt so good in his, so *safe*. With an almost visible effort, she pulled herself together. The sooner she was out of here, the better. She had literally been saved by the bell. If the telephone had not rung when it did, she would probably have embarrassed both Neil and herself by asking him, on the basis of their brief acquaintanceship, to fix an appointment for her to meet Viscount Haldane. *And yet*—the idea wasn't *all* bad. But she would have to follow it through alone when she had enough time to devote to composing a suitable letter. 'I—I hope I haven't got you into trouble with his Lordship.' She wasn't entirely joking.

Neil smiled. 'There's no problem. His Lordship and I get along very well.' He stood back and Kersty went to the door.

'He's lucky to have found someone who shares his vision and dedication.' She felt her colour rise even as she spoke, and wondered if she'd gone too far. But Neil's answering grin made her toes curl with delight.

He held the door open for her. 'There are definite perks to this job,' he murmured, his eyes dancing as he held her gaze. 'Such as rescuing beautiful girls who come trespassing on Sunday afternoons. Though it's not something I would wish to make a habit of.'

'Nor I,' she replied, recognising the warning beneath his light tone. 'Today was—exceptional.'

'I shall take that as a compliment,' he grinned.

Kersty shook her head in mock amazement. 'The arrogance of some people! You'll never be lonely, Neil, not with that ego for company.'

He lifted one hand and touched her cheek, gentle, almost tentative. 'You'd be surprised,' he said softly. 'Goodbye, Kersty. And use the main gate. No more fences.'

'Oh, yes—I mean, no,' she stammered. 'Bye, Neil.'

'Goodbye,' he'd said, not 'I'll see you again,' or 'Are you on the phone?' she thought to herself as she walked quickly down the drive, deaf to the birdsong, heedless of the spring sunshine warm on her face, or the sharp breeze.

Plunging her hands into her pockets, she tossed her hair back. Forget it, she told herself firmly. You are fighting for professional survival; there's no time and precious little energy left to waste on distractions, even when they are as attractively packaged as Neil Drummond. No, it was better like this.

She was still trying to convince herself three days later.

Kersty looked up from her drawing-board as Sue walked in from reception with the post. 'Any cheques?' she asked hopefully.

Sue shook her head. Her cropped auburn curls, hazel eyes and freckles were a vivid contrast to her apple-green baggy sweatshirt and white denim skirt. She had a soft, clear voice, a lilting Cornish accent and, despite her colouring, a wonderfully calm disposition.

Many was the tense situation she had defused when Kersty, burdened with business pressures plus her own artistic temperament, clashed with Josh's volatile personality.

Kersty often wondered how they would have survived without Sue's practical good sense and impish humour. She sighed.

'We've been pleasant, understanding and patient,' Sue announced, 'and it's got us nowhere. I think I'd better start threatening, apologetically, of course.'

Kersty frowned doubtfully.

'Nothing nasty,' Sue assured her, 'just...several reminders, no reply, greatly regret no choice but to put the matter in the hands of our debt-collection agency.'

Kersty's eyes widened. 'But we don't *have* a debt-collection agency,' she pointed out.

Sue waved one of the letters. 'We could have. There's a new one setting up in town. This is an enquiry about leaflets for a mail shot. We could come to some mutual arrangement. Shall I look into it?'

'Please,' Kersty nodded. 'Anything else that's urgent? Only I'd like you to do the typesetting for that Cook's Kitchens brochure as soon as you can. I asked around and they are good payers. Money on the dot. If we can get the copy and transparencies to Fred by the weekend, there's a chance we'll get it back before the end of the month.' She grimaced. 'If we're lucky.'

'We really should use another printer,' Sue remonstrated. 'Or at least spread the work around more.'

'Tell me something I don't know.' Kersty supported her chin on her palms. 'But I can't pay Tremayne's bill until we get the cheque in for that contract job for the Tourist Board. Besides,' she shrugged, 'where else would we find someone who gives us the quality Fred does, at his price? It's really too low. I don't know how he makes it pay at all.'

'He does it for love,' Sue grinned. 'He thinks you're wonderful.'

Kersty's head jerked up in astonishment. 'Sue, Fred is eighty if he's a day.'

'What's that got to with anything?' Sue asked innocently. 'You're only as old as you feel. And Fred has the body of a fifty-year-old and the heart of a lion.'

'Who on earth told you that?' Kersty demanded.

'*He* did,' Sue said, straightfaced. Then they both giggled.

'I'll make sure he gets *his* cheque at the end of the month,' Kersty promised drily. 'The copy is in the filing cabinet. I finished it last night.'

'What about the transparencies?'

'In an envelope clipped to the copy. By the way, what's Josh doing today? He was already in the dark-room when I came in from the meeting with Mr Edrich about the new guide-book. You were on the phone.'

Sue nodded. 'It was the secretary of the Flower Festival confirming arrangements for the video. I've put a note in with the post and marked the dates on the calendar for next week.' She placed two unopened envelopes and several sheets from a message pad on the bench near Kersty's drawing-board. 'How did the meeting go?'

Kersty shrugged. 'He was impressed with my ideas, but wasn't too keen on the price. We both know he'd be getting value for money and he wouldn't get better quality work anywhere else, but he has to go through the motions of haggling, I suppose. He said he'd phone in the next day or two.'

'Did he suggest lunch?' Sue grinned again.

Kersty's brows climbed. 'You're telepathic.'

Sue shook her head. 'No, I've just heard the rumours. Apparently he's got a wife who doesn't understand him.'

Kersty snorted. 'She probably understands him only too well. Anyway, I turned down lunch. Pleaded pressure of work.' She looked from her drawing-board, covered with rough sketches, to the bench strewn with paper samples, typed copy, colour charts, half-completed designs, Letraset and several copies of a design magazine. 'Which is no more than the truth. I've got more *work* than I know what to do with. What I need is *money*.' She smiled to soften the urgency.

Out in the reception the phone rang. Sue went to answer it and Kersty turned her attention once more to her drawing-board.

'One moment, please,' she heard Sue say. 'I'll just see if she's in.'

Kersty looked up. Sue put her hand over the receiver and mouthed, 'Miles Quintrell.'

Kersty tensed, and her first reaction was to shake her head. But almost at once she raised her hand to stop Sue saying anything. Reluctantly, she got down from her stool and picked up the extension.

Sue replaced her receiver, said 'Coffee?' and, as Kersty nodded, went into the typesetting-room which led to the tiny kitchen.

'Good morning, Miles,' Kersty said, and the calm confidence in her voice surprised her. She must be a better actress than she realized, for inwardly she was trembling. 'What can I do for you?'

'I'd say it was more a question of what I can do for *you*.' Miles's voice always made Kersty think of a sleek, well-fed cat. It had a sort of self-satisfied purr that grated on her nerves. 'Come and have lunch.'

'I can't today, Miles.' Kersty kept her tone pleasant with an effort. 'I'm terribly busy.'

'You still have to eat,' he pointed out with heavy joviality. 'Naturally, I'm delighted you have so much work. After all, our merger wouldn't otherwise have been contemplated. But time is getting on, Kersty, and my accountants are anxious to get the final details arranged.' The charm was still there, but thinner. 'Your creditors would hardly be delighted to learn that you had deliberately gone bankrupt rather than take advantage of my company's offer. A very generous offer, under the circumstances.'

Kersty's eyes flashed angrily and she bit her lip to hold back the torrent of words she longed to hurl at him. He was enjoying this. She could visualise the gloating expression on his face. He revelled in wheeling and dealing and the manipulation of power. He probably had a repressed childhood, she told herself in an effort to maintain at least a façade of calm.

'I do appreciate your dilemma, Miles,' she said sweetly, 'but it really is impossible.' A little demon made her add, quite untruthfully, 'You see, I already have a lunch appointment.'

'Then break it.' The veneer had cracked and Miles's impatience showed through.

'And lose business?' Kersty countered immediately, knowing full well he would hate *that*.

'Listen, Kersty,' his voice was tight with curbed irritation, 'you've had three weeks to study the figures. Your own accountants must have told you the deal is more than fair. And if they are working in your best interests, they will have advised you to sell out.'

There it was, from his own lips. He wasn't proposing a merger. No matter what he chose to call it, he was actually demanding total capitulation. Unfortunately, John, her accountant, had told her quite bluntly that if the business was to survive she had precious little choice but to accept Miles's terms.

Still Kersty resisted. She knew her stand was based on emotion rather than logic. Harry, Sue and Josh might not be aware of the seriousness of the situation at this very moment, but there was no way she could keep it from them for much longer.

Maybe tomorrow she would have to give in, admit defeat, and sign over three years of total commitment and hard work, three years of vision and creativity, to someone who could think only in terms of profit and loss. Of course, profit was a necessary consideration, but it wasn't the *only* thing that mattered. She knew with a sure instinct that Miles was jealous of her talent and was rejoicing at this opportunity to control it.

But not *today*. Twenty-four hours, that was all she wanted. One more day. It wouldn't make any difference to him, and somehow, something might turn up. Swallowing hard, she forced some warmth into her voice. 'I could make it tomorrow, Miles. Unless you're too busy, of course.'

'Too busy for lunch with my favourite designer?' The charm was on full-flood, and Kersty knew how it would feel to drown in melted marshmallows. 'How could you even think it?'

'Foolish of me,' she responded drily.

'I'll pick you up at twelve-thirty.' Miles was brisk, the organiser taking charge. 'I'll book a table at the Waterfront and tell them to make sure they have a bottle of their best champagne on ice.'

'A real celebration,' Kersty murmured.

Miles missed the irony completely. 'But of course.' She could hear the smirk of satisfaction in his voice. 'And not before time,' he reproved. 'You really have drawn this whole business out an awful lot longer than necessary.' Then he added magnanimously, 'Still, all's well that ends well, as they say.'

You smarmy, conceited, cliché-spouting hack, Kersty wanted to shout. She was gripping the phone so tightly that her knuckles ached. Suddenly, she couldn't stand it any longer. 'I must go, Miles. There's someone in reception waiting to see me.'

'Not half as impatiently as I am.' The words slid, smooth and facile, from his tongue.

Her mouth curling in disgust, Kersty put the phone down hard, and looked up to see Sue holding two coffee-mugs.

'I don't know why you talk to him.' She handed a mug to Kersty who leaned against the bench, staring down into the steaming liquid. 'You can't stand the man.'

The smell of the coffee transported Kersty back to Sunday afternoon, Neil Drummond's living-room, Brazilian coffee, 'black with one spoonful of sugar', cherry buns served on expensive china, the scent of applewood as flames licked the logs in the fireplace. She thought of the handkerchief, now washed and ironed and folded neatly in her bag. She would have to post it to him. She should have done it sooner. It too was obviously of high quality. The little crown embroidered in white in one corner instead of an initial had intrigued her. She would have liked to ask him about it, tease him even, accuse him of delusions of grandeur.

She deliberately blocked the train of thought. There had been no word from him since. She might as well forget Sunday. Pretend it never happened. It had been a brief and all too pleasant interlude, nothing more. 'Beggars can't always be choosers,' she murmured.

'What are you talking about?' Sue was clearly puzzled. 'Miles Quintrell is competition, isn't he? We can do without the likes of him, snooping around.'

'I only wish that were true.' Kersty clasped her coffee-mug in both hands. She hadn't meant to reveal so much. 'What I mean is,' she explained carefully, 'Miles wants to discuss a proposition that would make quite an improvement to our income.'

'Mmmm.' Thoughtfully, Sue raised her mug to her mouth.

'And in business, if you aren't going forward, you start slipping back,' Kersty added.

'Josh doesn't like him either,' Sue said. 'And Harry—what Harry thinks of Miles Quintrell isn't repeatable.'

'Good,' Kersty's tone was tart, 'because none of *you* has to deal with him or make the decision. Aren't you lucky? The responsibility is all mine.'

'Don't forget the post,' Sue said mildly. 'There's one marked personal, so I haven't opened it. By the way, you asked about Josh. He's editing the wedding video to get it out of the way so he's free for the Flower Festival. He thinks that could take two days.' Sue's face glowed with pride. 'He got some fantastic shots at that wedding. The bride looked absolutely fabulous.' She giggled. 'There are a few really candid ones of the reception, people gossiping and other folks trying to be pleasant to people they can't stand. Honestly, it's *hilarious*. Give me a shout if you want anything. I'll take Josh and Harry their coffee, then as soon as I've done the letters, I'll start on that typesetting.'

'Thanks, Sue,' Kersty grinned. Her flaring temper had burned itself out as it always did in the face of Sue's equanimity. 'How are you going to manage at *your* wedding? If Josh is busy being the bridegroom, he can hardly be filming it as well.'

'Don't count on it.' Sue grinned. 'Knowing Josh, he'll come up with a brainwave, like *you* doing it.'

Kersty shook her head. 'I intend to enjoy the day, not be fretting about angles, and light and all that stuff.' Finishing her coffee as Sue disappeared into the typesetting-room, Kersty put her mug down on the bench and picked up the post. She made a practice of reading everything that came in. Sue was already dealing with those that needed answers, the rest would be filed.

Tearing open the long, buff envelope, she saw, with a sinking sensation, that it was a reminder from Tremayne's. She read it quickly, then stuffed it back into the envelope. At least *they* hadn't reached the stage of making threats.

Kersty had always prided herself on paying her bills promptly, and it rankled that she was unable to do so now.

She picked up the cream envelope. The paper was thick and had a textured finish. It was addressed to her personally in bold handwriting and black ink. Not recognising either the writing or the distinctive stationery, she opened it, unfolded the sheet of matching paper, and gasped.

Kersty didn't even breathe as her eyes flew down the page, then returned to the top to read the words once more. She needed to reassure herself they really did say what she thought they said.

'I don't believe it,' she whispered. 'I just don't believe it,' she repeated, her voice rising with excitement. 'Sue,' she shouted, still staring at the creamy paper now trembling in her hands. 'Sue! Josh! Harry!'

The door to the typesetting-room was wrenched open and Sue shot out into reception. 'What's the matter?' Her eyes were wide, her expression concerned.

Josh's wiry form clad in sweatshirt and jeans, his dark hair an untidy mop, appeared next, followed by Harry's stocky figure, shirtsleeves rolled up as usual.

'What's happened? Is there a fire?' Josh demanded.

'Someone paid their bill?' Harry quipped, realising the news was good rather than bad.

'Always the wise guy,' Kersty retorted, trying hard to control her excitement. She had to remember they didn't know just how critical the cash-flow situation had become, or how precariously the busines was balanced. They could not know just how much this opportunity meant.

'For God's sake, speak to us!' Josh pleaded. 'Is it good news or——'

'Listen,' Kersty cut him short. She took a deep, steadying breath and started reading aloud. 'Dear Miss Hurrell, your name has been brought to my attention as a graphic designer capable of producing a prestige brochure aimed at the top end of the market. There is also a strong possibility I shall require a promotional video as well. Should you be interested in discussing a package in which quality is of paramount importance, perhaps you would ring the number above to arrange an appointment. Yours faithfully,' she paused, 'I can't read the signature, but the address is Ravenswood. It's from Viscount Haldane!'

'Are you sure?' Josh was suspicious. 'It sounds almost too good to be true.'

Kersty thrust the letter at him. 'See for yourself. It's a printed letterhead.' She could barely contain her bubbling excitement. This was Neil's doing. It had to be. *That* was why she hadn't heard anything from him. It would have taken time to put the idea to Viscount Haldane, and convince him to at least interview her and discuss the matter. In fact, the more she thought about it, the more remarkable Neil's achievement became. How would she ever be able to thank him?

'It *looks* genuine enough,' Harry agreed grudgingly.

'Why shouldn't it be genuine, for heaven's sake?' Kersty cried. 'This is the best thing that's happened to us for months, though from the looks on your faces anyone would think you'd just been handed a ticking parcel.'

Josh shrugged. 'Sorry, it's just—how did he choose us? I know we're the best, but we're small fry compared with someone like Miles Quintrell.'

'He did specify *quality*,' she retorted. 'Miles Quintrell specialises in the mediocre.'

'And you're having lunch with him tomorrow?' Sue murmured so only Kersty could hear, her expression puzzled.

Kersty pretended not to have heard and kept her eyes on her brother. A grin stole over his face, widening his mouth and lighting his eyes. 'If this is for real...wow! It could really put us on the map. A commission like this...' He shook his head, eyes glazing as infinite possibilities floated through his mind.

'Just what *is* the commission?' Harry asked. 'What does his Lordship want us to promote?'

'Ravenswood House,' Kersty answered without thinking. 'It's being turned into a luxury private hotel.'

Three heads turned towards her. 'How do you know?' they demanded in unison.

Hoping they would put the sudden heat in her cheeks down to excitement, Kersty shrugged. 'It's all over the village. I'm surprised you haven't heard.'

'You'll have to arrange some money up-front,' Josh warned. 'If this Lord What's-his-name wants a really first-class job, some of the filming will have to be done from the air. If he's aiming to push privacy and seclusion as a selling point, aerial views of the house and the setting are a must. So that means hiring a helicopter. The interiors will be no problem. I suppose he'll want the gardens shown as well, and maybe the park——' He had grabbed a pad and pencil from the bench and was scribbling furiously as ideas occurred.

'Hold it, Josh.' Kersty laid a restraining hand on her brother's thin shoulder. Younger than her by four years, he was six inches taller, thin, and surprisingly strong. He ate hugely, loved chocolate, yet burned up nervous energy at such a rate that his weight never varied. 'I'd better go and see him first, to find out what he has in mind, before we start on a storyboard.'

'So, what are you waiting for?' Josh's impatience was legendary, except when he was working. Then no detail was unimportant, no effect too much trouble. 'There's the phone.' He pointed, then added as an afterthought, 'What about this deal with Miles?'

Deal. Her head jerked up. *How did he know?* She swallowed.

'I was just telling Josh about you having lunch with Queasy Quintrell when you shouted,' Sue explained. Kersty managed to hide her relief. 'Will you still go? Much as I loathe the man, he does have a lot of useful contacts. And I don't suppose we can afford to turn down business, not yet, anyway.' From her tone it was clear she wished they could, at least as far as Miles Quintrell was concerned.

Grimacing, Kersty nodded. 'Yes, I shall still have lunch with Miles.' The very thought of it made her stomach tighten, for she would have to stall him, play for more time. She dared not tell him what he could do with his takeover bid until she was absolutely sure of the Ravenswood job. It would be a meeting fraught with difficulty.

Kersty shivered. She had a horrible suspicion her fight to retain her business was only just beginning.

Retrieving the letter from Harry, she took several deep breaths, but still her heart thumped. Watched by three pairs of eyes reflecting her own excitement, anticipation and hope, she picked up the phone and began to dial.

CHAPTER THREE

THE WINDSCREEN wipers clicked busily and Kersty slowed the little car to a crawl as she made her way gingerly along the rutted and pot-holed drive. It probably made sound economic sense to put off the long-overdue repairs until the diggers and heavy lorries had departed for good. But, in the meantime, visitors to Ravenswood faced a very uncomfortable ride.

Last night's forecast had mentioned the possibility of scattered showers. It had not warned of a monsoon. She sighed. Cornish weather had always been a law unto itself, probably due to having the sea on three sides of the county.

So much for the two hours she had spent the previous evening cleaning and polishing her ancient red Mini so as to create a good impression. She might as well have saved herself the trouble. The downpour had turned stiff earth and dusty pot-holes into mud-puddles which splashed their contents upwards to streak the wings and doors as she lurched towards Ravenswood House.

She had entered the estate from the road at the top of the village, bumping over the cattle grid as she passed the tiny lodge. Though she still could not see the house, hidden as it was behind the trees, she knew she was almost there.

Nervousness clenched her stomach into a solid knot. The outcome of this afternoon's meeting with Viscount Haldane was more than important now, it was vital after what had happened yesterday during her lunch with Miles.

She had tried. She had been bright and witty and amusing, passing on news and titbits of mild gossip about mutual acquaintances in the design world. She had asked after Caroline and the children, listening attentively and making admiring noises as Miles proudly listed their various accomplishments. It had all been for nothing. He had known at once what she was up to, only she hadn't realised it then.

She had been horribly tense even before the meal began. The champagne he insisted she drink had burned like acid. Though she barely touched her food, pushing it around the plate while she encouraged him to talk, by the time coffee arrived she had painful indigestion.

Miles added cream and two sweeteners to the dark, fragrant brew, then sat back in his chair, his eyelids heavy as he studied her. 'All right, Kersty.' He sounded bored. 'Playtime is over. You're trying to stall. I don't know why and I really couldn't care less. But I want an answer, and I want it now. Just tell me the deal is on. We'll go to my office, sign the papers, and put an end to all this time-wasting.'

For a moment she considered trying to bluff it out. But only for a moment. A glance at his thin mouth warned her against it.

As she hesitated, her mind racing, a smirk of satisfaction began to twist his mouth and crease the pouches under his eyes. Smugness oozed from every pore. I've got you, he seemed to be saying.

All of a sudden Kersty was staggered to hear her own voice announce calmly and with perfect clarity, 'You're absolutely right, Miles. Too much time *has* been wasted. The answer is no.'

She had not known she was going to turn him down, until the words actually came out. But as soon as they did she felt a great weight slide from her shoulders. It wasn't logical, of course. In fact, she was taking a terrible risk. The pressure to solve the cash crisis and reestablish the business on a firmer foundation would be intense. Yet she could not conjure a single regret. She had worked day and night, sweated blood, and shed many bitter tears to get it going. It had cost her dearly in more ways than she cared to number, but it was *hers* and hers it would stay.

Miles's mouth hung open. His shock was total. Kersty felt an instant's fierce pleasure. He had been so *sure*.

He recovered swiftly. His teeth met with a snap. His eyes were sharp with malice. 'I don't find your idea of humour particularly amusing.'

'I'm not joking, Miles,' she replied evenly. The terrible tension that had strained her nerves almost to the breaking-point had melted away. Strength and resolve poured like adrenalin through her veins. If you believed, *really* believed in something, then you fought for it. And she was ready to fight to the last breath in her body. 'I'm not selling out, to you or anyone else. I set up K. Graphics. It's mine, and that's the way I intend it to stay.'

'Oh, very heroic,' he mocked. 'But haven't you overlooked something? You can't afford it. You're overdrawn at the bank, you owe your suppliers, and if Fred Morrison didn't have a soft spot for you...' He broke off abruptly and Kersty knew he'd said more than he intended. Had Miles approached Fred to try and persuade him to stop printing for her? Thank God he hadn't succeeded, for that really would have been the end.

Kersty wasn't looking for a fight, so she didn't follow up his inadvertent disclosure. 'It would be pointless to deny the facts,' she said, still calm. 'You made a fair offer, Miles. But I am at liberty to refuse it, and that's what I'm doing.'

A look of cunning crept across his puffy features. 'You've got someone else lined up,' he accused softly. 'You're trying to play us off one against the other.'

'The idea never occurred to me,' she said truthfully. 'Miles, I'm not selling to *anybody*. I'm going to work my own way out of this mess.'

His laugh was full of scorn. 'You'll need some pretty hefty commissions to pull you out of the financial hole you're in.'

She tried to keep her face expressionless. But Miles sensed something. She watched his face change. His features grew sharp. 'You've got something, haven't you?' he accused. 'You've landed a big one.'

Unable to prevent tell-tale colour warming her cheeks, Kersty managed to hold her gaze steady. 'I told you before, Miles. I have more work than I know what to do with.'

'Dime-a-dozen stuff,' he scoffed.

She bit her tongue, longing to hurl a list of her recent credits at him, but wise enough to know it was precisely this into which he was trying to provoke her. He wanted to force her into justifying her decision, to put her on the defensive. She must not fall for his tactics. She had to remain calm and aloof. It wasn't easy.

'I see you're not denying it,' he observed, his mouth curling in a sneer.

She stood up then. 'I'm under no obligation to confirm or deny anything. You made the running, Miles, you wanted this merger, I never did. But for a while I couldn't see any alternative.'

'And now you can,' he snapped, 'which can only mean one of two things. Either you've talked the bank into extending your overdraft, or you've managed to wangle an important commission from a wealthy client. I know which sounds more likely to me.'

Digging her nails into her palms, Kersty shrugged. *She would not be goaded*. But her nerves were tightening again. 'You will believe whatever you choose to believe, regardless of anything I say.'

'You're so right.' Miles stood up, glaring at her. 'My company is the largest in the area. No one can match the range of services Duchy Design has to offer.'

'Then you haven't a thing to worry about, have you?' Kersty retorted sweetly.

'Who's worried?' Miles sneered. 'I'm just curious as to why a makeshift little outfit like yours has been offered this plum job. You can't afford to drop your prices.' He smirked again. 'What's the gimmick? Are you offering... fringe benefits?'

Kersty felt herself grow pale. The insinuation was unmistakable. Her self-control teetered for an instant as several lacerating rejoinders trembled on her tongue. He was the dregs. She drew in a slow, deep breath and composed her face into an expression of mild puzzlement. 'I really don't know what you're talking about, Miles. As for my "makeshift little outfit",' she mimicked his scorn, 'only a few minutes ago you were anxious to buy it. Please excuse me, I've rather a lot do do. Thank you for lunch.'

'A total waste of time,' he muttered sourly. 'I can't even say it was a pleasure.'

Kersty flashed him a brilliant smile. 'Chalk it up to experience, Miles. You can always claim it on expenses.'

'This isn't over yet, Kersty,' he scowled. 'I don't give up that easily.'

Once more she curbed an almost uncontrollable desire to lash out verbally. Choking back anger and frustration, she nodded politely. 'Goodbye, Miles. I'll see myself out.'

The pains in her stomach had continued for several hours and Kersty wondered, not for the first time, if she could be getting an ulcer.

Now, as she followed the curve of the drive, she took one hand from the steering wheel, pressed her fingers just under her breastbone and wished the burning sensation would go away. An ulcer at twenty-five was just too ridiculous to contemplate. It was nerves, that was all.

She passed the entrance to a paved yard which had outbuildings on two sides and a high stone wall on the third. Sounds of hammering and sawing, accompanied by a transistor tuned to the local radio station, issued from doors and windows open in spite of the rain.

A few yards on she drove between two tall stone gate-posts, beneath an archway of trees, and cut on to a huge gravelled semicircle that fronted the house.

Kersty hesitated for a moment, torn between leaving the Mini where it was, barely a yard from the steps to the front door, and being accused of thoughtless parking, or moving the car back to the neatly trimmed hedge and getting soaked on the thirty-foot run to the porch. She heaved a sigh and opted for good manners.

The wheels spun on the gravel as she tucked the Mini up against the hedge facing the way she had come in.

Quickly checking her appearance in the driving mirror, she pushed a stray curl back into her upswept hair-style. Its rich mahogany sheen showed to best advantage when it hung loose, curling in heavy waves on her shoulders. But putting it up made her look not simply *older* but somehow more mature, more authoritative. Needing all the help she could get, there had been no choice. Up it had gone.

She had limited her makeup to mascara, to darken the tips of her thick lashes and enhance her green eyes, a touch of blusher and some coral lip-gloss to counter her nervous pallor and give her face some much-needed colour.

She had been equally careful in choosing what to wear. She needed to make a good impression, but she also needed to feel confident enough about her appearance to be able to forget it and concentrate entirely on pro-moting her abilities as a graphic designer capable of handling a prestigious account. To do all this she *had* to be comfortable, which ruled out skirts and high heels, items she possessed but rarely wore.

After an hour spent trying and discarding various outfits from her wardrobe, she had decided on a pair of smart black trousers, low-heeled black patent pumps, and a batwing-sleeved top of black, coral and emerald.

Battling with portfolio, bag and umbrella, she made a dash for the lofty granite porch. Leaving her umbrella, still open, in the corner to dry, she brushed the few drops of rain from her trousers, smoothed her hair in a tell-tale gesture of nervous anticipation and, grasping the darkly tarnished bell-pull, tugged hard. It came off in her hand.

Kersty's breath caught in her throat as she stared at it in horror, then, hearing a sound, glanced up at the door.

At least ten feet high, it was newly painted and the deep maroon gloss had a mirror finish. Kersty could see her reflection, a picture of guilt. She looked at the door-knocker. Of smooth, highly polished brass, it matched the door-knob and letterbox.

Grasping her bag and portfolio more tightly, she transferred the broken bell-pull to her other hand and lifted the knocker. The resounding thud made her flinch.

Almost immediately the door swung open, silent on well-oiled hinges. A man in his mid-thirties wearing the uniform of a butler inclined his head and said pleasantly, 'Good afternoon, Miss Hurrell. Please follow me. His Lordship will be with you in just a moment.' He stood back, waiting for her to enter.

Kersty had been mentally rehearsing her opening words, who she was and why she had come, so his greeting threw her off balance. 'Oh. Th-thank you,' she stammered. She stepped inside.

He closed the door with barely a click. 'Would you care for some tea? Or perhaps you would prefer coffee?'

Despite her nervousness, Kersty was impressed. But she was so tense she couldn't face either. 'No, thank you. Not just now. Oh—er——' Lifting her hand she held out the broken bell-pull. 'I'm terribly sorry. It—I——'

'Don't give it another thought, Miss Hurrell,' he said as he took it from her. 'It's due to be mended next week.'

She followed him across the patterned carpet. A small, bare reception desk stood unobtrusively in one corner. Kersty was vaguely aware of ivory walls, white paintwork, subtle lighting and lots of plants. The overall impression was one of warmth and welcome.

Passing a glass door, Kersty glimpsed armchairs and sofas upholstered in pink, grouped around low tables on a carpet of clover-green.

They came to another door, white-painted and panelled. The butler opened it and motioned her inside. 'Please make yourself comfortable. His Lordship will be with you directly.'

A nervous spasm clenched Kersty's stomach and dried her mouth. She backed into the room. 'D-do you think I might have a glass of water, please?'

'Certainly, Miss Hurrell. I'll fetch it at once.'

'It's very kind of you.' She smiled tentatively.

'Not at all.' He smiled back. She knew he recognised the fact that she was nervous, but there was nothing condescending or patronising either in his smile or his manner. She watched the door close behind him. It couldn't be easy, being a butler, she mused. It was rather like middle management, the boss on one side, the staff on the other, and you having to keep both happy. It was also a job involving service, a concept which seemed to have gone out of fashion, and required total control over emotions and expression, not to mention a degree in diplomacy.

Yet there was nothing remotely *servile* about the man who had just left. He had been pleasant and polite, but in no way familiar. In fact, now she came to think about it, he had been far more at ease with her than she with him. But that had nothing to do with rank or class. He was secure in his job. She, on the other hand, was not.

Unless she made a favourable impression on Viscount Haldane, her whole future, and that of the others back at the studio, was in jeopardy.

She dropped her bag on to a chair, leaned her portfolio against it, then turned to face the room. Her eyes widened, taking in Wedgwood green walls, apricot carpet, and furniture gleaming with the rich patina of age. Two sofas faced one another on either side of a white Adam fireplace, and comfortable armchairs in muted shades invited company. Though the rain still poured down, light streamed in from two long velvet-draped windows.

Kersty's head moved slowly in admiration. Everything she had seen so far reinforced her impression of casual elegance and understated luxury. Despite the obvious quality of the furnishings, the house was not simply a showpiece; it welcomed, soothed and offered comfort in an atmosphere of peace and calm.

She crossed to the nearest window and looked out, wondering what it must be like to live permanently in such surroundings. She supposed the Viscount simply took it for granted. Beyond the gravelled path, smooth lawn, broken only by clusters of azalea bushes, each a profusion of white, yellow, scarlet and pink blossoms, stretched nearly fifty feet to a low stone wall. At one side, tall rhododendrons formed a windbreak and screen. Beyond the wall more lawn, dotted with trees and shrubs, sloped down to a fence separating the garden from the park.

Conjuring pictures of ladies in crinolines and parasols taking tea on the grass, Kersty was aware of the door opening and, assuming it was the butler returning with her water, spoke without turning round. 'It must be enormously satisfying, working in such a beautiful place.'

'It is,' a voice replied, a deep voice touched with quiet laughter. *Not the butler's voice.*

Startled, Kersty swung round, her cheeks burning with embarrassment.

'Oh,' she gasped, relief flooding through her. 'Neil, you made me jump.'

'I'm sorry,' he smiled.

'No, it's all right. I'm so glad to see you.' Realising she sounded more enthusiastic than might be wise for only a second meeting, she lowered her eyes then looked up at him once more, frowning slightly. 'You're all dressed up.'

He glance down. His dark suit was expertly tailored and fitted him perfectly, subtly enhancing the width of shoulder, narrowness of hip and length of leg. He raised his hand to the knot of a maroon and grey striped tie, held in place over a pale cream shirt by a plain gold tie-pin.

'It's only a suit, Kersty,' he mocked, 'not the Crown Jewels.'

She felt warmth return to her face. 'You know what I mean.'

'That I look more at home in jeans and workshirts?' he queried, straightfaced.

'Yes—no—you're a rotten tease, d'you know that?' She hissed at him, her glance darting towards the door.

He nodded solemnly, then openly studied her. 'You look quite different too, with your hair up like that.'

She shrugged, her nervousness showing. 'I have to try and look the part.'

He moved towards her. 'What part is that?'

She lifted one shoulder. 'Older, mainly. I have to appear the type of person who can run a successful business, be organised and capable, and still have creative flair.'

His brows climbed. 'And for that you must look *older*?'

The ghost of a smile tilted the corners of her mouth. 'If I want to be taken seriously by someone who doesn't already know me. When I left college I had just completed a four-year course in Graphic Design, and graduated with honours. I've run my own business ever since and I'm not boasting when I tell you I'm good at my job. But I'm only twenty-five. And if I had a pound for every time I've been patronised or chatted up by men who can't see beyond the fact that I'm young and female, I'd be a millionaire now.'

'Oooh!' He winced softly. 'That sounds bitter.'

She shook her head. 'I'm not bitter, just irritated.' His expression was doubting. 'Honestly. And I'm tired. I wouldn't have to go through all this if I was a man.'

Neil's smile was cryptic. 'Who said life was fair?'

'You're right,' she allowed after a pause. 'I really shouldn't complain. Things might not be easy, but I'm luckier than most. I have a job I adore. How many people can say that? Anyway, what I really meant to say was, thank you for setting up this meeting for me with Viscount Haldane. I really am grateful. The idea—well, the possibility had crossed my mind after we'd talked, and I thought of asking you then, but it seemed an awful cheek. I mean, we'd only just met. It wasn't as if you knew me or my work.' Sensing that her tongue was beginning to run away with her, and might let slip more than she intended, Kersty stopped. She rubbed her hands together awkwardly. 'Anyway, thanks.'

Neil gestured towards one of the sofas. 'Shall we sit down? How is your back, by the way?'

Kersty glanced at the sofa uncertainly, and remained standing. 'It's fine, almost healed. Look, Neil——'

'Did you see a doctor?'

She shook her head. 'I sloshed on some TCP and masses of antiseptic cream when I got home. I even managed to put a plaster on, though I nearly stuck it to the mirror. It was more to save my clothes than to protect the wound.' She went pink. 'I think your first aid was really all that was necessary. And to be honest, I really couldn't spare two hours to go and sit in the doctor's waiting-room.' She glanced at her watch and her frown was a mixture of worry and irritation. 'I wish his Lordship would hurry up. My appointment was for eleven. It's ten past now. *He's* probably got all the time in the world, but I shall be working until nine tonight as it is. In fact, I'll probably be working till nine for the foreseeable future, especially if I don't get this job.'

'Why?' he demanded curiously.

Kersty bit her lip. 'I've done something totally illogical and financially crazy.'

Neil gazed at her. His eyes narrowed. 'You've turned down the merger?'

She nodded. Her gaze slid, uneasy, to the door. 'Neil——'

'Why?' he repeated.

She shrugged. 'Call it a brainstorm,' she answered flippantly. Then, hugging her arms around her body, she turned once more the the windows and looked out. 'No, it wasn't,' she murmured. 'It was the best move I ever made.' She glanced round at him, an impish smile tilting her mouth and lighting her eyes. 'Not the wisest, perhaps, but definitely the most satisfying. I wish you could have seen Miles's face. He was all gloat and smirk, playing me like a fish on a line. He was absolutely *stunned* when I told him I wouldn't sell. He just couldn't believe it.' Her smile faded and she stared out of the window once more. 'I don't regret what I did. I know it was *right*. But life certainly won't be easy for the next few months.'

'But surely, if you get this job for Viscount Haldane——' Neil began.

Kersty turned to face him, clasping her hands in front of her. '*If,*' she said. '*If* I get it. Of course it would make a tremendous difference.' She grinned. 'Not to mention the knock-on effect of a commission from a member of the aristocracy. It's almost as good as "By Royal Appointment".' Her face grew tense, serious. 'But I'm not counting any chickens. On the few occasions I've depended on something, I've always ended up wishing I hadn't.'

'Some*thing* or some*one*?' Neil queried softly.

Kersty pretended she hadn't heard. Her eyes flickered towards the door yet again. 'In any case, I've no idea how many others he'll be interviewing. I know I can compete favourably with Duchy Design and Concept...' Her chin lifted a fraction. 'If you want the truth, I could wipe the floor with both of them. But if he's thinking of looking outside the county...'

'I don't think you have a thing to worry about,' Neil smiled, his voice warm and gentle.

She raised her eyes, met his steady gaze, and felt a strange constriction around her heart. 'You *are* kind,' she blurted, colouring. 'I wish——' She stopped, checked her watch again, and looked at the door. 'Where *is* he?'

'Kersty, I——' Neil began, taking a step towards her.

'I know,' she interrupted, raising both her hands to forestall him. 'You have to go.' He kept on coming. 'I've taken up far too much of your time. You're dressed so smartly, I'm sure there are all sorts of important things you should be doing.' He was right in front of her now. Only inches separated them.

'Well, actually, there is one,' he agreed, and as Kersty looked up at him, puzzled, his strong hands cupped her face and his mouth covered hers. His lips were warm. They caressed hers, exquisitely gentle, they teased, they coaxed. Then tenderness blossomed into passion. Neil caught his breath, his lips pressed down on hers, parting them, and Kersty, her head swimming, heard a soft answering sound drawn from her own throat. She had been kissed many times in her life, but never, never had it been like this. His mouth kindled a flame deep within her and, as he stroked her face and throat, her skin was quiveringly alive to his touch. His body brushed hers and they both swayed.

Then he tensed and she felt him fighting for control. Reluctantly, he dragged his mouth from hers and, lifting his head, stared deeply into her eyes.

Kersty felt dizzy. Her breathing was quick and shallow. Her knees had turned to water and her heart pounded against her ribs like a prisoner in a cage.

His gaze searching, Neil's expression was troubled. 'Forgive me, Kersty,' he muttered. Grazing her cheek lightly with his lips, he released her and turned away.

She did not understand. 'It wasn't exactly unpleasant, Neil,' she smiled, feeling oddly shy, yet at the same time wanting to dance and sing for sheer joy.

Caution, her head warned, but her heart refused to listen. After Martin, she had built a wall around her inner self, so grievously hurt she had wondered if recovery was even possible. At the time it hadn't mattered for she had not cared. *Never again*, she had vowed.

Immersing herself in work, she had avoided all relationships except, of necessity, those connected with business.

Yet slowly, unaware, she had healed. Neil's kiss was the first in a very long time, the first ever to evoke such strange, wonderful feelings. Her blood fizzed in her veins like champagne.

Neil glanced at his watch and turned to face her. 'I wasn't referring to the kiss,' he said quietly. 'I make no apology for that. How could I, when it's something I wanted to do since the first moment I saw you?' He pushed his hands into his trouser pockets. There was an uncharacteristic hesitancy about him. 'Kersty, I'm afraid——'

'Look, it's all right, I do understand,' she interrupted, recalling his surreptitious look at his watch and wanting to make it easier for him. He had already taken time out to make her feel more relaxed, but it was clear from his clothes that he was due somewhere other than the woods. 'I am grateful, Neil.'

'Gratitude wasn't exactly what I had in mind,' he said drily.

'No.' She coloured swiftly. 'I—I meant about this,' she gestured, 'the interview. I'm not half so nervous. In fact, by the time I've finished, ever so modestly of course, I'll have convinced Viscount Haldane he's lucky to get me!' She flashed him a warm, happy smile.

But Neil did not respond. 'Kersty, you *don't* understand, there's some——'

There was a discreet knock and the door opened at once to admit the butler. He was carrying a silver tray on which rested a silver coffee service, a plate of chocolate biscuits and a glass of water.

Neil cursed under his breath and, catching the tone rather than the actual words, Kersty's eyes widened as her gaze flew from Neil to the butler and back.

'Thanks, George,' Neil's voice was expressionless as he nodded to the butler who set the tray down on an antique table.

George bowed, picked up the tumbler and offered it to Kersty. 'My apologies for the delay, Miss Hurrell.' He clearly did not intend to give a reason or make excuses. Kersty had a feeling that if the cooker blew up or the chef went berserk, George would announce in the same polite, measured tones that 'dinner will be subject to a short delay.'

'That's all right. Thank you.' She took the glass carefully and, suddenly uncertain, glanced up at Neil, who pushed a hand through his hair in a gesture of impatience and resignation.

Kersty raised the glass and sipped the ice-cold water. Something had changed. The atmosphere in the room was different and she didn't know why.

'Leave it, George.' Neil's peremptory tone, as the butler began to pour the coffee, startled Kersty, adding to her unease. 'I'll see to it myself.'

'As you wish, My Lord.'

Kersty choked on the mouthful of water and began to cough. Setting the glass down quickly, her eyes streaming as she gasped for breath, she pulled a tissue from her sleeve and held it to her mouth.

Both men turned towards her, their expressions concerned.

'Are you all right?' Neil asked.

She nodded, unable to speak, swallowing convulsively. She *couldn't* have heard—her mind was playing tricks. George *couldn't* have called him——

George turned to Neil. 'My Lord, I did not wish to disturb you, but Mr Tregonning has telephoned twice. He needs a decision concerning the joists in the small barn.'

'And naturally, it could not wait until lunch time,' Neil commented acidly. He was immediately brisk and businesslike. 'Ring him back and tell him to replace the two at the far end. The rest will be OK with treatment. And tell him I want the lintel over the door replaced with precast concrete. The existing one looks more like lace than wood.'

'Yes, My Lord,' George bowed. 'Do you intend visiting the site this afternoon? Doubtless Mr Tregonning will ask.'

Weariness flitted across Neil's hard features. It vanished almost at once, but Kersty had glimpsed the constant, driving pressure and her heart contracted in sympathy. Immediately, she banished it. What a joke he'd been having at her expense. How he must be laughing inside. And how long would he have continued the pretence if George had not, in all innocence, blown it wide open? Anger flared, swift, hot and bitter, and she had to hold it under tight control. *She had trusted him.*

'I'll be on site at four,' Neil stated.

'Very good, My Lord.' George withdrew, closing the door quietly.

Neil turned to Kersty. He stood straight and very tall, his face devoid of expression, his eyes slightly hooded so she could not read them. 'Coffee?' he suggested.

Crumpling the tissue in a clenched fist, Kersty glared at him, lips compressed, head and heart at war. 'That was a *rotten* thing to do,' she burst out.

'Oh, I don't think so,' Neil responded mildly. 'George often relays messages when I'm otherwise engaged. Alf Tregonning is quite used to it.'

'Don't play games with me,' Kersty fumed. 'That's not what I'm talking about and you know it.'

'Do sit down and have some coffee,' Neil cut in. 'You did say you were short of time, so the sooner——'

'Stop ordering me about!' Kersty snapped. 'Who the hell do you think you are to——' She stopped herself with a half-embarrassed, half-bitter laugh. 'Daft question. I know who you are—*now*. But *you* didn't tell me.' Her voice fell and the hurt was clearly audible. 'You cheated. You lied to me.' What a fool she was. She should have know better.

'No, Kersty.' His response was immediate and emphatic. 'Don't say that. It wasn't intentional.'

'Then why didn't you tell me?' she cried. She knew she was wrong to allow the hurt to show. She should have bottled it up inside and got out of the house as fast as she could. By letting him know that it mattered, she had handed him a weapon.

He raised an eyebrow in cynical weariness. 'And if I had, would you have talked to me, confided in me, the way you did? I rather doubt it.'

Kersty's angry glare faltered, and her thick lashes fluttered down to veil her eyes. He was right, of course. But

as some of the things she had said out in the woods and
here in this elegant room only minutes before sprang to
mind, hot colour rose like a tide up her throat to flood
her face. She winced in an agony of embarrassment. *She
had called one of his relatives a nutcase. She had told
he had an outsize ego. She had criticised the aristocracy
in general and the owner of Ravenswood in particular.*

Her anger died, leaving her empty and confused.
Clasping her hands together so tightly that they hurt,
she lifted her head. Her small chin jutted, part bravado,
part defiance. Whatever else he might label her, she
wasn't a coward.

'My Lord, I must apologise——'

'Kersty, Kersty,' he mocked gently. 'Spare me that.
Not formality, not from *you*.' Her colour flared and her
chin lifted a fraction higher. He took a step towards her,
but caught himself and stopped.

The air between them seemed to shimmer, full of a
tension new to both. 'I'm still Neil Drummond, the chap
who unhooked you from a barbed-wire fence and ad-
ministered first aid.' His eyes gleamed. 'Primitive,
perhaps, but effective. After all, what do you expect from
a man who spent five years in the Brazilian jungle—
finesse?'

Kersty didn't smile. How many times had she relived
that moment, the touch of his hands and mouth on her
back? Never in her life had there been anything to
compare... *until he kissed her*.

But now he was suddenly a stranger, not the man she
had thought. No wonder she had sensed something different about him, the slight remoteness, the air of
authority.

She wrenched her attention back as he went on, 'I've
been thanking my lucky stars ever since that you had
enough spark to ignore the "Keep Out" notices.'

'Really?' Defensiveness and uncertainty made her voice sound cool. 'Whose cottage did you take me to? And how long did you intend to continue the deception?'

The light faded from his eyes leaving them opaque, unreadable. 'The cottage is my home. It's where I live,' he said flatly. 'This house, beautiful though it is, is business as far as I'm concerned, and I like to leave business behind at the end of the day. As for the other, it was not a deliberate deception. If you recall, it was you who assumed I worked on the estate. As a matter of fact, I do. I work damned hard.' His tone was cold. 'I had been trying for several minutes before George came in to...'

'Tell me the truth?' Kersty supplied acidly.

'I had not lied,' Neil snapped. 'I was trying to *explain*, but you thought I was trying to leave.'

Kersty looked down, biting her lip.

'I wanted, foolishly, perhaps,' his voice held a bitter self-mockery that unexpectedly tore at Kersty's heart, 'to be accepted for what I do, rather than who I am. I thought—I hoped you were different.'

Her head came up quickly.

'It seems we've wasted rather a lot of time. I think we'd better get down to business. When can you start?'

Kersty stared at him. 'You...you mean...I've got the job?'

He nodded briefly.

'Don't you want to see some examples of my work?'

'Have you done anything on this scale before?' he demanded.

'Well...no...' she admitted.

'Then it wouldn't really help, would it?' He stood up suddenly and, pushing his hands into his pockets, strode to the window and stared out. She turned on the sofa and watched his profile; it was hard and closed. A chasm had opened up between them. She knew she was partly responsible and grieved for what had gone. Yet what choice had she had? He had not been honest with her.

'With so much money invested,' he said quietly, still gazing out of the window, 'the presentation is of vital importance. I want it in the hands of someone I can trust.'

'B-but you hardly know me,' Kersty blurted. 'Aren't you taking a terrible risk?'

Neil turned. He gazed at her long and hard, his expression deeply thoughtful. 'Hardly know you? I wouldn't say that, Kersty. I wouldn't say that at all.'

CHAPTER FOUR

THE REST of the day passed in something of a haze. Josh took one look at Kersty's smiling face as she arrived back at the studio, and dashed into the tiny kitchen. He re-appeared brandishing a bucket containing crushed ice and a bottle of champagne.

Kersty was both surprised and delighted. 'Where did you get that?'

'From the fish shop in the High Street.'

'Not the ice, you idiot, the champagne.'

'I nipped into the Wine Cellar while you were out.'

'Weren't you taking rather a chance?'

Josh shook his head. 'Couldn't lose,' he said confidently. 'If you got the job, we'd celebrate. If you didn't,' he shrugged, 'we'd drown our sorrows.'

Sue hurried into the kitchen to rinse the coffee-mugs. Josh lowered the bottle for a moment and draped an arm over his sister's shoulders. 'Glad you made it, kid. We're pretty close to the edge, aren't we?'

She glanced up quickly.

'Don't flannel me, Kersty,' he warned as she opened her mouth, the automatic denial already on her lips. 'You've been showing definite signs of strain this past few weeks. Still,' with a final squeeze he released her and raised the bottle once more, 'the odd little job like this should brighten the picture a bit, eh?'

She nodded, grinning. 'Just a bit.'

Clutching coffee-mugs full of chilled, sparkling wine, Harry, Josh and Sue perched on any available surface around Kersty and excitedly demanded to know, word for word, all that had happened.

Kersty described in detail what she had seen of the house and grounds. Then she gave an edited version of what had been said. She wasn't quite sure why she omitted anything which gave even the slightest hint of a personal relationship between Neil and herself. Perhaps it was the same reason she had said nothing about her clandestine excursion to Ravenswood on Sunday and its outcome.

She had not been involved with a man for a very long time. Too long, in the view of both Josh and her father. And, despite the magnetic attraction of Neil Drummond, she was not sure she wanted to be, even assuming he had any such inclination. Besides, he was not what he had seemed. And, while she had felt a growing affinity to Neil Drummond, Viscount Haldane was something else altogether.

So, forced as she was to refer to him as 'his Lordship' or 'Viscount Haldane', Kersty found no difficulty in sounding quite objective. The title itself lent formality and detachment to her résumé of their discussion concerning the brochure and video.

But even as she talked, her delight and excitement about the job visible in her glowing cheeks and shining eyes, a pensive corner of her heart wondered if the man she had known only as Neil Drummond was lost to her for ever.

It had been Neil who had tended her back, who had talked about the woods, who had drawn out of her things she had never spoken of before. Neil who had held her face in his hands and kissed her, awakening feelings she had been unaware she possessed.

Her reaction had driven that part of him back behind a cool, patrician façade which, during the remaining half-hour of her visit, had encased him like an invisible armour.

He had been polite but businesslike. He had asked pertinent questions and listened thoughtfully to her answers. But of the man she had teased and laughed with there was no sign. Not once in that half-hour had he used her Christian name; in fact, he had not addressed her at all. His handshake as she left had been brief, and she had hurried through the rain to her little car with an aching sense of loss.

It wasn't her fault. There was no escaping the fact of who he was. It could hardly be ignored. He was surrounded by servants. He had a fleet of people working for him. Even the architect was anxious that every detail should meet his Lordship's approval. He was treated by everyone with a deference that set him apart. *Everyone but her.*

Even as embarrassment burned once again, she recalled his harsh, bitter crack about thinking—hoping she was different.

Before she had realised exactly who he was, there had been...something. She had glimpsed a solitariness about him, a separateness that struck an answering chord in her. She understood all too well the burden of responsibility. Had she been too hasty in her condemnation of his behaviour? Yet what could they possibly have in common? She was growing more and more confused.

When the last of the wine had been swallowed, Sue dropped the cork into Kersty's bag as a memento of the biggest commission they had ever undertaken. Then they returned to work, each aware of the need to clear jobs outstanding in readiness to begin the Ravenswood project.

At ten minutes to five Mr Edrich phoned. Kersty took the call and listened to the phoney regret as he said that unless she lowered the price it would be difficult for him to recommend K. Graphics for the guide-book. Her face set as he went on to allow that there were several points on which compromise might be reached, and perhaps they could discuss it over dinner?

Kersty let him go no further. As Sue tried, unsuccessfully, to stifle a fit of giggles, Kersty told him she was sorry they wouldn't have the privilege of working for him. But they could not lower the price without sacrificing quality, and as quality was the foundation on which the business was built, she could see no possible solution. It appeared he would have to look elsewhere. She totally ignored his suggestion of compromises and dinner.

'Why not try Duchy Design?' Kersty suggested sweetly. 'Ask for Miles Quintrell. I'm sure you'll both get along splendidly. You have such a lot in common. Good afternoon, Mr Edrich.' He was still blustering, telling her not to be so hasty, when she put the phone down.

That night it was almost ten when Kersty arrived home, exhausted, but oddly content. Her faith in her own ability had been justified, and her decision to turn Miles down vindicated. That alone was enough to make her feel buoyant. But there was more to the slow, deep stirring of anticipation than the creative ideas that were beginning to bubble in her head. Some time very soon she would be seeing Neil again. She was startled to realise she still thought of him as Neil, and even more surprised at how much she was looking forward to that moment.

Josh and Sue had left the studio at nine to go for a Chinese meal. Harry had stumped off soon after, warning Kersty not to stay too late.

Over scrambled eggs and two cups of tea eaten at the kitchen table, Kersty recounted the events of the day to her father.

Stanley Hurrell sucked on an old and much-loved pipe as he listened, taking the stem from his mouth occasionally to blow a plume of smoke. He rubbed the polished bowl with long, sensitive fingers that betrayed the artistic streak inherited by both his children. Head of the music department at the town's comprehensive school, he was also musical director of the Boscarrick Male Voice Choir.

'You're sure this chap is sound, Kersty?' His tone contained an element of doubt.'

'What do you mean, Dad?' she asked, puzzled. 'He is who he says he is.' She got up and took her plate, cup and saucer to the draining-board. 'There's no doubt about that.' Her voice was tinged with irony.

'I was thinking more along financial lines,' her father said. 'Kersty, this sounds like a very big job, and you are a very small company. Don't get me wrong, love. I don't want to spoil your pleasure. I just don't want to see you bite off more than you can chew.'

'Yes, it's big, Dad. But we can handle it. I have a great team.'

Her father was not to be easily put off. 'It's a hard world, Kersty, and there are some hard people in it. A title doesn't guarantee moral behaviour. The upper classes can be quite peculiar about money. Remember the Carvossas——'

'Dad, that was *years* ago,' Kersty broke in.

'Maybe. But will he pay up, this Viscount Haldane? That's what I'm asking. You've already had two bad debts, and look at the damage they did. A third, especially on the scale you're talking about, could write off your business. I'm concerned for you, love, that's all.'

Kersty patted her father's shirtsleeved shoulder as she leaned across the table to pick up the tray. 'Actually, I put that to him myself. Not quite as bluntly, of course. But I did ask if he had any idea of the cost of a project such as the one he had in mind. He said he didn't imagine it would be cheap.' Recalling the dry tone and raised eyebrow, Kersty felt a quiver inside and went on quickly, 'I told him a rough estimate for a fifteen-minute film, with voice-over commentary and music, plus the brochure, would be in the region of twenty thousand pounds.'

'What did he say to that?' her father asked.

'He just nodded, said it was about what he thought, and he expected a first-class job, especially as he'd heard such glowing reports of our work.'

'He'd heard about you, eh?' Her father looked pleased. 'Who from?'

Kersty grimaced. 'Actually, it was from me. Before I knew who he was. I—it's a long story, Dad, but basically, just a case of mistaken identity. Anyway, I told him that we didn't know how to do anything less than a first-class job.'

Stanley Hurrell nodded. He puffed on his pipe for a moment or two, then asked curiously, 'What's he like?'

Kersty ran hot water into the sink, added a squeeze of washing-up liquid and kept her back to her father as she dabbled her fingers in the lather. 'To look at?' She paused for a moment, not because it was an effort to remember, but because two images occurred at once, filling her mind, so vivid that her breath caught in her throat. One, a tall, powerful man in denim shirt and jeans, a shotgun over his shoulder, and a gleam in his eyes. The other, the same man, dark-suited, aloof, unapproachable. The images superimposed, blending, separating and blending again. And Kersty realised it was pointless to ask which image was the *real* one. They both were. Two facets of his job, two sides of his personality. 'Tall,' she blurted, suddenly aware of the length of her silence. 'In his mid to late thirties, I suppose. Darkish hair streaked by the sun. Apparently he spent five years in Brazil.'

'I meant as a person,' her father said thoughtfully.

'He's well spoken, courteous. He has beautiful manners. He made me feel——' *terrified, breathless, exhilarated . . . alive* 'quite the lady,' she finished lamely. 'You would call him a real gentleman, Dad.' *A gentle-*

man. And so he had been. That kiss... But that was only part of the story. There was more, something stronger, darker, more ruthless. The man that had survived the Amazon forests. And even that was not all. 'He's...' she hesitated, trying to put what was only a feeling, intuition, into words. 'He's quite a mixture,' was the best she could manage. 'He runs the whole estate himself. He has staff, of course, but he's the one in overall control. He has a degree in forestry as well.'

'What about his wife?' her father asked. 'Did you meet her, too? What's she like?'

A newly washed plate slipped from Kersty's hand and crashed heavily on to the draining-board. 'He's not married,' she threw the words lightly over her shoulder, scrubbing hard on a pan. 'Apparently, Mrs Laity goes in once a week to cook, clean, and do the washing.'

'Only once a week? A place that size?' Stanley Hurrell was openly astonished.

Kersty was about to explain that Neil didn't live in the house, but stopped herself in time. Explanations would only lead to more questions, and she had a strong feeling she'd said too much already.

Her father was studying her, frowning thoughtfully as he drew on his pipe.

'He seems to have told you quite a lot about himself,' Stanley Hurrell observed. 'More than necessary, I would have thought. Do I get the impression there's more than just a job involved here, Kersty?'

Relieved her father could not see the heat in her cheeks, Kersty attacked the pan with renewed ferocity. 'Honestly, Dad!' she chided, not looking round. 'I hardly know the man. You asked what he was like. I've given you as broad a picture as I can, that's all.' A flat denial might have been more convincing, but she had never been able to lie to her father, or to herself.

'Listen, love, don't fall for him. He's probably a genuine sort. He certainly sounds an enterprising young man. But with backgrounds as different as yours, it can only end in tears.'

Kersty wrung out the dishcloth with unusual force. 'I never thought you were a snob, Dad.'

He removed his pipe. 'I'm a realist, Kersty. We are ordinary people. That doesn't mean we are *less* than anyone else. We're certainly not stupid. But we're not gadabouts. Our families have lived in the county for generations. Your mother's family has been in this village for over a hundred years. From what you tell me, that young man has seen the world. He's used to a different way of life. It's my guess he won't stay long. He'll do whatever it is he's planned with the house, get the money coming in, then he'll move on.'

No, Kersty wanted to shout, you're wrong. He cares about Ravenswood. It's not simply a business opportunity. He's putting down roots, establishing a future for his children.

She moistened her lips. 'That's not the impression he gave me,' she said carefully. 'And, to be honest, Dad, your argument sounds more like old-fashioned class-consciousness. A ''Them and Us'' attitude. I thought that had gone out with the ark.'

Her father's look held a sympathy that made her wonder if he had seen through her charade of objectivity.

'No, love. Sadly it hasn't. But I'll say no more. You're a grown woman. Old enough to live your own life and make your own judgements. Just don't get hurt.' *Again.* He didn't say it, but the implication was clear.

Kersty wiped her hands on the towel and dropped a kiss on her father's forehead. 'I've won an important commission, Dad. The only thing that concerns me right now is doing the best possible job, and getting paid.'

Stanley Hurrell puffed silently on his pipe and picked up the evening paper.

Late the following afternoon, Kersty sat alone in the studio. Sue was working on the typesetter. Harry had finally tracked down the faulty connection in one of the machines and was fixing it, while Josh put the finishing touches to the storyboard which gave them a graphic display of how the Flower Festival video would be put together.

The reception area was empty and classical music issued softly from Kersty's small cassette player. She sat at her drawing-board, her hair caught back in a loose ponytail, totally absorbed as she made sketch after sketch, trying out ideas for the presentation of Ravenswood.

The sound of a gentle cough penetrated her concentration, and she looked up.

Neil stood in the studio doorway watching her, tall, tanned, and immaculate in a light grey suit, striped shirt and plain tie.

His silent arrival was such a shock to Kersty that she simply stared at him. He had been so much on her mind. To look up and actually see him made her wonder, just for an instant, if he was a figment of her imagination.

That illusion was swiftly dispelled as he stepped into the studio and glanced around him. 'You are obviously busy, so I won't hold you up.'

She pulled herself together at once. *How long had he been there?* 'No, it's all right...I just...I didn't expect...actually,' she confessed in a rush, 'I thought I was dreaming.'

His brows climbed and Kersty's face grew hot. She hurried on, 'I mean, I didn't hear the door, or you come in, or...anything.'

There was no smile on his mouth, no gleam of warmth in his shadowed eyes. His face was unreadable, as if he had deliberately wiped all expression from it.

Kersty felt a constriction in her chest. It shouldn't matter. They were virtual strangers. Last night she had reasoned it all out and convinced herself she didn't want the inevitable complications of a man in her life, particularly *this* man. Now all her careful reasoning counted for nothing.

Neil opened his jacket and reached to an inside pocket. 'We didn't discuss the financial arrangements in detail at our last meeting. I thought, under the circumstances, you might find this useful.'

Acutely sensitive to every nuance, Kersty recognised the reprimand for having doubted his ability to pay. She glanced at the cheque, looked again, felt herself pale, and raised wide eyes to Neil. 'Five *thousand*?' she murmured.

His features tightened imperceptibly and Kersty registered, but did not understand, the air of strain about him. 'Isn't it enough?'

'Yes. Oh, yes,' she nodded, breathless. She could pay Tremayne's, the suppliers, and Fred, then clear the overdraft—well, part of it—and still have enough over to get the project off the ground. 'Thank you.' Her smile, heartfelt and dazzling, was a blend of relief, gratitude and sheer pleasure at seeing him again, a pleasure she could no longer hide.

Neil Drummond's jaw clenched. All his life his relationships with women had been uncomplicated by any emotion stronger than mutual attraction and affection. Partings had never grieved him, and pleasure had been a thing of the moment, untrammelled by plans for a joint future.

But this girl...ever since he had heard her cry for help and stepped through the bushes to see her trapped on the wire, he had been unable to get her out of his mind. She was different. There was something about her, an honesty as refreshing as iced lemonade on a hot day. She had been hurt. The wariness deep in those candid eyes bore mute witness to past pain. But there was strength too, and humour, and an impulsiveness against which, he guessed, she constantly battled.

That first day he had thought...had hoped... He cursed himself for a fool. Perhaps if he'd managed to tell her himself—who was he kidding? Her face said it all. She no longer saw the anonymous man in the woods. It was the money, the saving of her business, that lit up her face with that beautiful smile, not him.

He gave a mental shrug and let cynicism harden around him. She wasn't different at all. She was just like all the others, blinded by his title and her own preconceptions. He'd be the aristocrat she expected, and to hell with damn-fool dreams.

Kersty half rose from the stool. But there was no answering smile from him, no thaw in his manner. He remained aloof and impersonal. And, as bitterness thinned his sensual mouth, cold fingers tightened around Kersty's heart. Her smile faltered and died.

The door to the typesetting-room opened and Sue bustled out, her arms full of fresh copy. 'Kersty, what do you want me to do with——' Seeing Neil, she stopped. 'Sorry, I didn't realise——'

He glanced briefly towards her, his smile courteous but distant. 'Please don't apologise. I was just leaving.' He turned to Kersty, now on her feet. 'When may I see the preliminary sketches? I would like to be kept informed at every stage.'

She stiffened, momentarily uncertain. 'I—that isn't the way I normally work.'

'Perhaps not,' he agreed blandly. 'But I think you'll allow that this situation is somewhat...unusual?'

Kersty caught the soft inner flesh of her lower lip between her teeth. It couldn't be that he didn't trust her, or that he doubted her ability. If so, he would never have given her the job. Besides, he'd just handed her a cheque for five thousand pounds on account. It was quite obvious there were already enormous demands on his time and energy. So why did he want to be involved in *her* work?

At that very moment Neil Drummond was asking himself precisely the same question. He had been startled to hear his own voice making the request.

Their eyes met. And locked. A current as potent as a high-voltage electric shock arced between them. Kersty's skin tingled and her mouth was suddenly dry.

For an instant Neil appeared deeply shaken, but recovered almost at once. His gaze flicked briefly to the cheque, met hers again, and one dark brow lifted fractionally.

Kersty's chin came up. 'He who pays the piper?' she challenged, her voice unsteady.

His eyes narrowed, glittering and dangerous. 'Quite so.' He started to turn away, but stopped and looked back at her over his shoulder. 'There is another reason.' His voice was harsh with self-mockery. She waited holding her breath. 'This is a new experience for me. I—there's a lot to learn.'

Kersty swallowed. *Could he possibly mean...?* She moistened her lips, her smile, uncertain, hope tightly reined. 'You and me both.'

His gaze was hard, probing. 'Then you'll ring me?'

Her hesitation was infinitesimal. She nodded and sensed an easing of the tension in him.

'I'll look forward to it.' His tone and manner were polite rather than warm. But the polished façade did not include his eyes. They were full of words as yet unsaid, of much to be explored, and Kersty's heart flipped over.

'Goodbye, for now, Miss Hurrell.'

'Goodbye——' She hesitated. She could not call him Neil again, not yet. Too much had happened and there was too much unresolved. As she opened her mouth to address him by his title, he flashed her a cutting look, part frustration, part warning. She felt weak and breathless, and wanted to laugh. Then, acknowledging Sue with a nod, he crossed the reception area in three strides and closed the outer door softly behind him.

Sue sagged dramatically against the studio doorway. 'What was all *that* about?' she gasped, her eyes sparkling with curiosity. 'Who *is* he, for heaven's sake? Kersty? Hey!' She leaned forward. 'Come in number seven, your time is up.'

Kersty started. Her heart was still pounding and there was a strange, hollow excitement in the pit of her stomach. She strove for a light, teasing note, not wanting Sue to guess how deeply Neil's request had affected her. 'You mean you don't know?'

Sue began to shake her head. 'How could I? I've never seen——' She froze, her hand flying to her mouth. 'Oh, Kersty!' Her voice dropped to an awed whisper. 'It wasn't . . . was it?'

'Who?'

'*Him.* You know.'

'If you mean our new client—yes, it was.' Her heart kicked.

'He's *gorgeous*,' Sue breathed, then, heaving a sigh, she hugged the copy to her, her expression thoughtful. 'I'll tell you something, though. For all his money and his title, I wouldn't swap him for Josh.'

'Any special reason?' Kersty was curious.

'Despite Josh's temperament, underneath he's as steady as a rock. He loves me and he makes no secret of it. But I get the feeling with that one,' she nodded towards the door through which Neil had disappeared, 'he's all locked up inside himself.'

'How can you possibly tell?' Kersty demanded, half amused, half irritated.

Sue snorted. 'You only have to look at him. You can practically *see* the wall. I suppose it's protection. I mean, how else does someone like him survive? People gawping at you every time you go out. You're on display the whole time. You can't scratch or swear or walk away when someone is boring you to death.' She shuddered. 'Who'd want it? Still, I suppose he's used to all that. It's a bit like royalty, really. They're born to it, aren't they? Never known any different.' She turned away and placed the copy in a tray on top of the filing cabinet.

Kersty moved slowly back to her stool. Neil *had* known different. His time in Brazil had not been spent in the cities, rubbing shoulders with people as sophisticated and cosmopolitan as any in London, but in the Amazon forests. His title would have meant little to the Indians and labourers. To them he would have been just another white man, a boss to be respected or cheated, depending on their mood and the power of his personality.

That was the man she had met in the woods. The man to whom she had been so strongly and unexpectedly attracted. And, despite everything, *still was*.

'Right,' Sue announced, 'I'm off now.' She pulled on her anorak and picked up the bundle of letters for the post. 'Nothing else you want, is there?'

Kersty shook her head. 'No, thanks. See you tomorrow.'

After Sue had gone, Kersty settled at her drawing-board. The presentation was coming together well. She had narrowed the possible approaches down to three, and had sketched each one of them in greater detail.

It was often easier, when she was working on a new project, to stay on after everyone else had gone. The building was quiet, the phone didn't ring, and there were no callers to disrupt the flow of ideas.

So why couldn't she concentrate? Dropping her pencil, she rubbed her forehead with the tips of her fingers, stretched her back and drew in a deep breath.

But as she looked once again at the drawings, all she could see was Neil's face. *This is a new experience for me.* The words echoed and re-echoed in her head.

She made herself a cup of coffee and went back to the stool, clasping the mug in both hands, watching the evening sun stream into the reception area.

Had he meant the packaging of Ravenswood, or his relationship with her? Could she even call it a relationship? They had only met twice before today, and that first time she hadn't known who he was. But now she did. And her anger at his apparent deception had melted and disappeared.

It was no use pretending the title made no difference. She found herself wishing fervently that he was plain, ordinary Neil Drummond.

She smiled wryly to herself and gazed at the steaming coffee. With or without a title, there was nothing plain or ordinary about the tall, brooding man who had kissed her, arousing a hunger whose strength she found unnerving. He had awakened feelings in her no other man had ever touched, feelings she hadn't known she possessed.

Despite her own initial doubts, despite her father's warnings, she wanted to know Neil Drummond. She wanted to hear about his family, his childhood, the people he knew, the places he had visited. She wanted to know his favourite music, his taste in food, the books he liked.

This is a new experience for me. Well, it was for her too. And she didn't know how to handle it. She gulped the coffee, her hand unsteady.

If she read him right, he had, in that statement, made the first move to bridge the yawning chasm that had opened up between them. Now it was her turn. She stared at the phone, torn.

He'd asked her ring him. It had been *his* idea. But would he expect to hear so soon?

She sucked in a deep breath. This was ridiculous. Placing her cup firmly on the bench, Kersty wiped a suddenly damp palm down the side of her jeans, and picked up the phone. Her pulse hammered loudly in her ears as she dialled.

She heard it ring and clutched the receiver with both hands.

There was a click, then George's voice said, 'Ravenswood House.'

'Oh!' Kersty cleared her throat. 'Good evening. May I speak to Viscount Haldane, please?'

'I'll see if his Lordship is at home. May I ask who is calling?'

Kersty swallowed. 'It's Miss Hurrell, Kersty Hurrell . . . about the project,' she added as a last-minute excuse.

'Just one moment, miss.' The line went dead.

Doubts crowded in. Kersty took the receiver from her ear and started to replace it. There was another click and Neil's voice came down the line. 'Hello?'

Kersty hesitated. His voice sounded flat.

'Kersty? Are you there? Don't you hang up on me.'

Relief coursed through her, leaving her legs shaky. She hitched one hip on to the bench, pressing the receiver to her ear. 'How did you know?'

'Intuition.' She could hear exultant laughter in his deep voice and it warmed her.

'That's a woman's prerogative.'

'Who says?' he challenged. 'I've been expecting this call for the past half-hour.'

Kersty closed her eyes. 'You could have rung me,' she pointed out.

'No,' he said softly. 'It had to be your decision.' There was a moment's silence, then, 'Where are you?'

'In the office.'

'Problems?'

'No. Everything's fine.' *Everything is wonderful, marvellous, fantastic,* her heart sang. 'But it's easier to work in the evenings, quieter.'

'I know what you mean. I'm sitting here surrounded by paperwork.'

'I thought you didn't take work home with you.'

'I don't. I'm in my office. It's just off the hall behind the reception desk.'

A vivid image of the imposing house rocked Kersty's new-found confidence. She was suddenly uncertain. 'I— I'm sorry. I didn't mean to interrupt——'

'For God's sake, don't apologise,' Neil broke in. 'I'd far rather be talking to you than preparing figures for my accountant.'

'You would?' Kersty blurted in delight, then, blushing furiously, tried at once to cover her pleasure. 'Still, if you don't like paperwork, even talking to the coalman is a treat.'

'He's a very pleasant chap, our coalman,' Neil said blandly. 'Breeds canaries. You still have the edge, though.'

Kersty grasped the receiver more tightly. 'I—I was wondering—the reason I rang—you did say you wanted to be kept informed...'

'That's right, I do.' His reply was swift and warm.

'Well, I thought... maybe you'd like to come in and look round the studio, see how everything is put together.'

He didn't reply at once, and Kersty felt a dampness under the heavy fall of hair at the back of her neck. She wiped it away with her free hand.

'I'd like that very much. The only thing is, I won't be able to manage it before the end of next week. Is that all right with you?'

'Yes, that's fine.' Kersty caught sight of her face in the small mirror attached to the notice-board. Her smile stretched almost from ear to ear. She wrinkled her nose at her reflection, poking fun at her own transparent pleasure. 'I've rather a lot on myself during the first half of the week.'

'Are you going to the Flower Festival?'

'Yes. I'll be doing interviews while Josh concentrates on the filming.'

'Fine. I'll see you there, then.'

Kersty couldn't hide her surprise. 'Are you going? I'd have thought you were too busy. In any case, it doesn't seem your thing somehow...' She clapped a hand over her mouth. She had no right to make such sweeping statements. What did she have to go on, *except intuition*?

'Just between ourselves, you're right. But I have no choice. I'll have to be there.' There was a rich undertone of amusement in his voice. 'You see, I'm performing the opening ceremony.'

Kersty gave a strangled gasp.

'See you on Wednesday. Think of some interesting questions.'

'Questions?' she croaked.

'You'll have to interview me, Kersty. I'm the guest of honour.'

She could hear him laughing as he put the phone down.

CHAPTER FIVE

KERSTY'S feet ached. She hadn't sat down since seven that morning, and it was now almost two o'clock. Even the ham sandwich and plastic mug of coffee which constituted lunch had been eaten on the move as she followed Josh among the exhibits.

The huge marquee was filling up. The heady scent of flowers and swelling babble of conversation were overpowering, and tension wrapped a tight band around her skull.

Trestles, raised in three tiers, edged the canvas walls and formed an island down the centre. Neatly covered in white lining paper, they groaned beneath the weight of vases, bowls and buckets, all crammed with luxuriant blooms of every hue. The whole tent was a riot of colour and perfume.

Mindful of the unseasonal warmth as well as the need to present a good front for her business, Kersty had discarded her usual jeans and sweatshirt for smart black cords and a lilac silk overshirt caught by a violet leather belt. Her hair was tied back with an emerald and lilac scarf.

Behind the clipboard she clutched like a talisman, she carried a black leather bag containing her lipstick, car-keys, purse, Neil's handkerchief and some spare fibre-tip pens. The cassette recorder and microphone with which she had already taped two interviews hung by a long strap from her other shoulder.

Part of her yearned to be out of the crush, far from the noise, the cloying sweetness of the flowers, and the heavier, more pungent odour of sweating bodies as the sun beat down on the canvas, warming the rapidly staling air.

Momentarily, she longed for escape. Yet her thoughts flew, not to the beaches and rugged coastline bordering the town, her recent refuge from people and the pressures of work, but to the lake at Ravenswood.

As a child, Kersty had been enchanted by the lake. Edged by a narrow path, fringed with reeds and marsh marigolds, shaded by towering beeches and graceful willows whose boughs curved and dipped to touch the mirror-smooth surface, it had seemed a magic place, not of this world.

At the far side, where the hillside rose so steeply from the water's edge that it was impossible to walk there, giant ferns grew and water lilies formed a thick, glossy islet.

She had always held her breath as she crept beneath the arch of rhododendrons which hid the path from all but those who knew where it led.

She had not seen the lake for years. Did the tiny, thatched summer-house with its open front and single semicircular seat still stand at the curve of the path? It was unlikely. The summer-house would be a rotted ruin, the lake silted up and choked with weeds. Nothing stayed the same. Childhood memories were special, but one had to move on. Yet, despite the years between, Ravenswood had not lost its magic, its lure. Only now it was not simply the park, woods, and lake that invaded her imagination, it was their owner.

She sighed, coming out of her reverie with a start as Josh called impatiently, 'Before or after, Kersty?'

'What?' She hadn't heard a word he said.

'The interview with his Lordship, are you planning to do it before or after the opening ceremony?'

'After. There won't be enough time before.' She glanced at her watch and excitement flickered through her like summer lightning. She tried hard to concentrate, to keep her mind centred on the filming and the schedule. It was impossible.

Dry-mouthed with anticipation, she looked about her. The noise and chatter grew as more and more people flooded into the tent in preparation for the opening ceremony. Neil's name was mentioned with increasing frequency, and Kersty found herself straining to catch snippets of conversation.

Much of what she heard was no more than idle curiosity, but a significant number of remarks contained resentment and hostility.

Two women stopped a few feet from Kersty, one complaining volubly about local people no longer having access to the fallen trees that had provided firewood for generations before 'this young upstart come down where he've no business to be.'

Kersty edged closer, pretending to study the notes on her clipboard, but the conversation had jumped to the other woman's impending operation.

Suddenly, awareness brought the fine hairs on Kersty's arms erect as a sixth sense told her Neil was somewhere nearby. For several seconds there was no change in the tone or volume of the babble. Then, like a ripple, the news spread to the furthest corner of the marquee. He had arrived.

'Get to the doorway,' Josh called to her across the heads of the people pushing forward and separating them. 'They're setting up a mike for him.'

Kersty pushed, elbowed and excused her way through the milling throng, emerging a few steps ahead of her brother, and found herself alongside the Outside Broadcast unit from the local TV station. Josh reached her side and raised the camera.

'This is terrific,' he grinned. 'I know it's not on the board, but a few feet of the TV people filming the event should go down well with the organisers.'

'Go easy, Josh. There's not much film to spare.'
Kersty's warning was automatic. Her brother had the
true artist's disregard for mundane matters like cost.
Quality and originality were all that mattered to him,
that special moment captured at the instant of happening or lost for ever.

Turning her head, Kersty saw Neil enter the marquee
and her heart gave a great leap.

Several inches taller than the knot of officials surrounding him, his dark head was bent forward as the
mayor, chain of office glinting, and two other men, all
hearty laughter and self-importance, vied for his
attention.

His expression one of polite interest, Neil nodded at
some remark, then raised his head and looked around,
apparently at random.

Kersty recognised the cool, bland façade, the pro-
tective barrier behind which the real man had retreated.
Hadn't she provoked the same reaction on learning who
he was?

For the first time in her life she comprehended the
enormous pressure of living in the public eye, and the
strength needed to deal with it.

Then, for an instant, his eyes met hers. They narrowed slightly, but not before she had seen the sudden
gleam. The corners of his mouth lifted in a smile so
fleeting that Kersty wondered if she had imagined it. He
was about to be swept past her. She had to warn him.

'My Lord.' Her voice was lost in the noise. She called
again, louder this time. 'My Lord, may I speak with
you?'

The mayor and dignitaries glared at her, huddling
closer around Neil, as if she presented a threat from
which they must shield him.

'Interviews will be granted *after* the ceremony,' one
man announced severely. 'You really can't expect...'

Kersty ignored him, her eyes never leaving Neil's. 'It is important.'

'That's what they all say,' another official muttered with ill-concealed irritation, while a third demanded of no one in particular,

'When will these young women learn to control themselves?'

'Gentlemen,' despite the bland expression, Neil's voice was unsheathed steel as his gaze swept over them, 'please excuse me for one moment.'

Kersty's admiration and respect for him rose even higher. He made no apologies or excuses. He did not explain or lose his temper. He simply stepped outside the circle and came to her side, bringing his head down close to hers, ready to listen to whatever she had to say.

Quickly, succinctly, trying to ignore the speculative looks and murmurs, she repeated the remarks she had overhead. 'I thought you ought to know *before* you made your speech,' she finished softly.

His expression didn't alter. 'Thank you,' was all he said. But the warmth in his eyes made her heart swell until she felt it would burst.

In two swift strides he returned to his entourage which closed about him like an amoeba.

Kersty's cheeks burned under censorious glances and she held her clipboard even tighter.

Neil stepped on to the small dais which had been hastily brought in and set up behind the microphone. There was a brief hiatus as the mayor and the organisers of the Flower Festival jockeyed for position and the local paper's photographer dazzled everyone with his camera flash.

Then the mayor introduced the chairman of the Festival committee, who in turn introduced Neil. After waiting for the polite clapping and whispers to die away, Neil began to speak. Josh raised the camera.

Kersty had deliberately positioned herself so she could see the audience as well as Neil. His deep, clear voice carried to every corner of the tent, and she watched curiosity about the man turn to absorption in what he was saying.

He did not use notes and his eyes roved constantly, moving from the people directly in front of him to those at the back and on either side, so that every person in the tent felt he was addressing them personally.

After paying tribute to everyone involved with the Festival, he switched smoothly to the subject of Ravenswood.

'Some of you will have been dismayed by the sudden withdrawal of privileges your families have enjoyed for generations.' There was a low murmur of agreement. 'Unfortunately, it is all too easy to forget that a privilege is not a *right*, and that because certain situations have existed for years, there is no obligation for them to continue.'

The muttering grew louder and feet shuffled restlessly. Kersty gazed at him in dismay. *What was he doing?*

'However,' Neil did not raise his voice, but the groundswell of noise subsided almost at once, 'Ravenswood is part of the village, and I would hope to see the village involved in its future, not just in terms of employment in the house and grounds, though we shall be recruiting staff quite soon.'

He had their total attention. 'I understand several of you have had difficulties finding premises in which to carry on crafts traditional to this village: furniture-making and boat-building.'

'What would you know 'bout that?' a sceptical male voice called from the crowd.

Kersty looked quickly at Neil. His mouth twisted in a wry smile. 'When you've made as many trips to the planning office and attended as many site meetings as I have been forced to do over the past year, it's impossible *not* to realise how many other people are facing the same strangling red tape.'

A roar of approval and agreement went up, and Kersty sensed a subtle but definite change in the attitude of the villagers. Though complete acceptance would take time, Neil was no longer an outsider. A glow spread through her.

'Several of the outbuildings near the main house have been converted into self-contained workshops,' Neil went on. 'There is seasoned wood available. Much of the timber now being felled is already contracted to buyers outside the county, but I am retaining some for sale locally. A replanting programme is planned, and dead or fallen trees will be available in logs or rings for firewood at a nominal sum.' Before anyone could ask how much he considered a nominal sum, Neil elaborated, 'I must cover the cost of sawing and transport, but I'm not looking for a profit, not on that, anyway.'

A burst of applause greeted his words, then, against a steady low hum of approbation, he pointed out that while a certain amount of change was both necessary and desirable, the heart of village life, the caring and sharing, was too important, too precious to neglect.

'Ravenswood is no rich man's toy.' His gaze swept each of them in turn. 'It is a way of life, and in order for all of us to benefit, it must remain healthy and profitable. I'd like you to be part of it.' Then, declaring the Festival officially open, he stepped back from the microphone to an enthusiastic ovation.

Hampered by her clipboard and bag, Kersty couldn't clap, but her smile said it all, or so she thought. She caught Neil's eye, but his face remained expressionless.

He stepped off the dais and came towards her. The entourage followed. 'I believe you wanted an interview?'

Unexpectedly, doubt stirred, like sediment in a pool, clouding her pleasure. Josh had the camera to his eye, lining up the shot, adjusting the focus and angle. The

mayor looked pointedly at his watch. Two of the organisers murmured disapprovingly, and all around people
stopped and stared, avidly curious.

'Miss Hurrell?' Neil prompted.

She searched his face, her nervousness deepening. The
beginning of a frown drew his brows together. There was
no special smile, no sign of recognition. They might have
been total strangers. Her throat dried, her mouth refused to work. She was paralysed by stage fright.

'Kersty!' Josh hissed. 'Get on with it.'

She swallowed painfully. *Why wouldn't the words
come?* Then she was elbowed aside and stumbled slightly
as the TV reporter, a brash young man with a toothpaste
ad smile, shouldered his way through, thrust a microphone under Neil's nose, and began questioning him.

Josh glared at his sister, then carried on filming the
interview. Hot with shame and confusion, Kersty backed
away, wanting only to lose herself in the anonymity of
the crowd. What had happened to her? How dared she
call herself a professional? She should have ignored all
the people and distractions and concentrated on Neil.
But he was the cause of her freezing. He had spoken to
her like a stranger.

Unable to stop herself, she glanced towards him. As
he answered the reporter's questions, he appeared perfectly relaxed, smiling, urbane; surely she couldn't be
the only one to see that he was seething with suppressed
anger? Yet, despite that, he was controlling the interview with an authority and professionalism which,
even as it evoked her admiration, sapped her remaining
confidence.

Apprehension reared up like a wave, ugly and threatening. *Was* she capable of handling Neil's project? Last
week she had been so sure. But now?

A hand on her shoulder made her jump. Warm,
clammy fingers gripped through the fine fabric of her
shirt. 'Why waste your time?' Miles murmured silkily,

his smile cold and sneering. He shook his head. 'What a performance, Kersty. If he was the ace up your sleeve, I'd say you've just crashed out of the game.'

Automatic denial leapt hot to her tongue, but before she could utter a word, Miles patted her arm, saying, 'I watched that pathetic little exhibition. Everyone can see you're way out of your depth. Go back to designing letterheads and leaflets for whist drives, and leave the top-league stuff to the real professionals. I bet you haven't even got a contract signed.' Tutting, he shook his head again and Kersty bit down hard on her lower lip as he swaggered off, angling through the knot of onlookers towards the tall man in their midst.

Kersty watched, horrified, unable to move. The reporter turned from Neil to the cameraman, and Miles, with plastic smile and hand extended, bull-dozed through and introduced himself. She saw Neil's expression harden for an instant, then he bent his head, frowning slightly, but clearly prepared to listen.

Kersty's whole frame sagged. She could guess what was happening. Miles might be a mediocre designer, but he was a brilliant salesman. On the day they'd had lunch, hadn't his parting shot been that he didn't give up easily?

She felt hollow, empty. Her performance today had given Miles exactly the opportunity he needed, and he was far too sharp a businessman to let it slip through his fingers.

But Neil had given her the job.

Would he stand by that after today's fiasco? After all, Miles's shot in the dark had hit the bull's-eye. *No contract had been signed.* With so much to do, she had not finished the costing and was still waiting for the hire-charge quote from the helicopter company. Neil was not legally bound to keep their agreement.

She turned away and started towards the entrance. Her forearm was seized and Josh jerked her round. 'What the hell's going on?' he demanded in a low voice that held as much bewilderment as anger. 'We had him on a plate, Kersty. Dammit, he couldn't have been more helpful.'

Tears welled in Kersty's eyes, making them shimmer. 'I know. It's all my fault.' Her voice cracked. 'First the interview and now this. I'm sorry, Josh. I——'

'Now *what*? What are you talking about?'

Wearily, Kersty indicated the two men, Miles still talking, hands gesticulating, as Neil listened, his face set and serious.

'Oh, *hell*!' Josh whispered furiously. 'How did he get in on it?'

'I'm sorry.' Kersty lowered her head quickly, unable to control the trembling of her mouth.

Touched by her visible distress, Josh put his arm around her. 'Hey, it's not the end of the world. So you blew the interview, so what? We can do it again.' He looked momentarily shame-faced. 'I'll need to use some more film, though. I caught his nib's speech and bits of the TV interview. I thought they'd be useful. As for the creep,' he glanced at Miles, 'just because they're talking, it doesn't mean anything.'

'You think not?' Kersty looked at her brother, her face drawn with self-reproach. 'Miles guessed we've got no contract. He's over there trying to cut us out.'

Josh paled. 'But surely his Lordship won't——'

'Why shouldn't he?' Kersty's voice wobbled. 'My performance will hardly have inspired him with confidence. I—I don't know if I can cope any more, Josh. Perhaps I've lost my touch. I——' She shrugged helplessly. 'I have to get out of here. I need some air.'

'Sure. Come on, I'll——'

'No.' She shook her head quickly, drawing away from him. 'I'll be all right. Honestly. You finish filming what's on the storyboard. Someone has to do the job properly.'

'Hi,' Sue appeared between them. She smiled happily up at Josh. 'I've been looking everywhere for you.'

He dropped a kiss on her upturned nose and grinned. 'How many times do I have to tell you? Try wherever the crowd is thickest.'

'Everything OK?' She glanced cheerfully from one to the other. Then, as she sensed the strain, her smile began to fade.

'Everything is fine,' Josh said briskly, giving Kersty no chance to speak. 'Now, grab that clipboard and come with me, Kersty wants some air. She's been stuck in here for hours. Between you and me, I think she's caught greenfly.' He winked encouragingly at his sister and hustled a giggling Sue away. Heads close together, he had one arm draped over her shoulders while the other hugged the camera. They disappeared into the crowd.

Keeping her own head lowered, avoiding eye contact with anyone, Kersty squeezed her way to the entrance and out into the glorious spring sunshine. Blinking at the sudden brightness, she sucked in deep breaths of fresh air. The breeze was cool. She longed for a drink to soothe her parched throat and throbbing head, but the thought of joining the queues at either the tea-tent or ice-cream van made her shudder. She hesitated, unsure of what to do next.

'Ah—Miss Hurrell, a word, if I may?'

The familiar deep voice tightened every nerve and brought her head up quickly. Hot colour stained her cheeks as Neil strode purposefully towards her, his little train of acolytes hurrying along behind.

Suddenly he stopped, turning to face them, a move so swift and unexpected that three men collided with one another. Despite the churning inside her, Kersty had to bite the inside of her cheek to mask a smile.

'Gentlemen.' Neil's tone was pleasant but brooked no argument. 'I am most grateful for all your assistance during the afternoon, but I feel I've monopolised you long enough. Doubtless you all have many demands on your time, and it would be inconsiderate of me to keep you from family, friends or other duties a moment longer. Thank you all.'

Thus dismissed, the men had little choice but to smile weakly, nod in agreement, and depart. They went slowly at first, then with increasing speed and intent.

'You can almost see them composing the headlines,' Neil observed softly, turning his head to watch the scurrying figures. '"In an exclusive conversation with Councillor So-and-so, Viscount Haldane today revealed his plans etc. etc."'

He swung back to her and she quailed at the bleakness of his expression. Then, as he passed a hand across his face, the mask slipped and she saw the lines of strain etched deep at the corners of his eyes and mouth.

'Let's get out of here,' he grated. 'The public's had its share of me for one day. We've a few things to sort out, you and I, and I'd prefer to do it without an audience.'

Kersty's legs filled with water and there was a tightness like clutching fingers in her chest. 'If—if it's about the interview, I'm dreadfully sorry. I don't know what——'

'We'll discuss it later,' he cut in brusquely. 'Right now, all I want is to get back to the cottage, have a long, cold drink, and get out of this suit. Come on.'

Helpless, swept along by the quiet power of his personality, Kersty found herself following him as he strode across the grass to the area roped off for the cars of the organisers, committee, and other VIPs. Her mind was in turmoil. He was like two separate people, and though intellectually she grasped the reason and need for the division, emotionally she hadn't yet come to terms with it.

From publicly treating her with the same distant courtesy as he had the organisers and hangers-on, suddenly the barrier was down and they were back to where they were. *But where was that?* Her footsteps slowed. It was all beginning to matter too much, and she was in grave danger of getting in over her head.

Neil glanced round. 'What's wrong? Don't worry about your car. I'll bring you back to collect it later.'

She gestured dismissively. 'It's at home. I walked down.'

He stopped and turned to face her. 'So what's the problem?'

'Neil, I don't—I can't——' She broke off as he smiled. It was the first genuine smile she had seen on his face that day, and her heart lurched.

His eyes were alight with laughter and his lips parted to reveal strong white teeth. The dark aura of strain surrounding him melted and vanished. He stook a step towards her. 'Now that's progress,' he murmured.

She was startled, bemused, then realisation dawned. She had instinctively used his Christian name.

'And if you apologise or try to deny what exists between us,' he said softly, 'I shall put my hands around your lovely throat, and shake you till you rattle.' He was still smiling, but there was undeniable warning in the deep blue eyes.

'Me deny it?' she retorted hotly, stung into retaliation, oblivious of how much she was revealing. 'You're the one who's been so—so——'

'Distant?' he supplied. 'Treating you exactly the same as everyone else?'

'Well...yes,' she admitted, uncertainty making her sound defiant.

'Oh, I *see*,' he nodded with exaggerated understanding. 'You're quite ready to have your name plastered all over the gossip columns. You're prepared for the speculation, innuendo and downright lies that will be printed the moment we openly admit our friendship. You won't mind being followed, watched, questioned and hounded, or your family and friends being grilled for every detail of your life and previous relationships.

Privacy will be just a vague memory, something other people enjoy. But if you're ready for all that——' He took her arm. 'Come on, we'll go back to the fray and let the local Press have their moment of glory, exclusive shots of Viscount Haldane with his latest mistress.'

'*No!*' Bewildered, horrified, Kersty snatched her arm free. 'You—they——' She blushed furiously. 'Anyway, I'm not your mistress.'

He arched a cynical brow. 'Do you imagine they'll believe that?'

'Why shouldn't they? It's the truth.' Embarrassment at her own secret thoughts and daydreams deepened her flush.

He sighed patiently. 'Kersty, don't be so naïve. Since when has the Press allowed minor irritations like facts spoil a good story?' His gaze darted beyond her shoulder. 'However, if you are serious about not wanting to be an overnight sensation, we really ought to get going.'

Kersty glanced round quickly. People were trickling towards the car park, arms loaded with pot-plants, flowers, cakes and bric-a-brac. She looked up at him, hesitant, vulnerable.

'What about you? Will you mind if they...?' She faltered, the words trailing away, not sure how to say it.

His shrug did nothing to ease her mind. 'It's an occupational hazard I've had to learn to live with. I'm thirty-six, unmarried, and I have a title. So gossip-column logic has it that if I'm not bedding every woman I'm seen with, I must have a suspiciously limp wrist.'

Eyes wide, Kersty gasped, then smothered a giggle. He leaned towards her, his eyes glittering. 'The truth is I've neither the stamina for the first, nor the inclination for the second.' He straightened up, pushing his hands into his trouser pockets as if to restrain himself from touching her. 'Kersty.' His voice was low, suddenly serious. 'I'm not concerned for myself. But you...it's only fair to warn you of what *could* be in store. Though this was neither the time nor the place I'd have chosen.' His grin was crooked. 'God knows, I don't want you frightened off before we've even had a chance——' He shrugged again. 'That's why I played it so cool. Now do you understand?'

Kersty's heart opened like a flower. Eyes shining, she nodded. 'Right.' She grinned up at him, light-headed with happiness, her headache completely gone. 'You're the expert in these matters. Do we strut, or do we scuttle?'

His eyes narrowed, full of secret promises. Kersty's skin tingled as excitement feathered along every nerve. 'We strut, definitely. Nothing catches the eye or stirs curiosity more quickly than furtiveness. The car's over there.'

She followed his pointing finger to a pale blue Jaguar Sovereign. The sleek lines and aura of latent power matched him perfectly.

Shooting him a sideways glance, trying hard to contain her exhilaration, she remarked, 'Nice little runabout.'

He shrugged, straight-faced. 'Short journeys don't suit the Lamborghini.' He opened the car door and held it while she got in.

The fine leather was soft and exquisitely comfortable. She lay her head back against the rest. 'Home, James,' she murmured happily, 'and don't spare the horses.'

Neil settled himself in the driving seat and switched on the engine. 'Comfortable?' he asked above the throaty purr.

Kersty turned her head. 'Blissfully,' she sighed, smiling. 'Anything to be off my——' He leaned across and kissed her hard. Though tantalisingly brief, the contact of his mouth, firm and warm, sent a shaft of sweet sensation through her. '—feet,' she finished shakily, and sat up straight in her seat, lifting the heavy fall of hair off the back of her neck, flushed with sudden heat that had nothing to do with the afternoon sunshine.

Neither spoke for a while. There was so much going on in Kersty's head, she was scarcely aware of the journey.

Neil drove fast but with the necessary care along the winding roads, and soon they were turning in at the estate entrance.

Kersty smiled to herself as he took one hand from the wheel, loosened the knot in his tie, and unfastened his collar. Though the suit fitted him superbly and he wore it with the ease and assurance of a man accustomed to formality, his preference for casual clothes was only too obvious.

Visibly more relaxed, he glanced at her. 'You're a fine one to laugh.'

Her cheeks pinkened. She hadn't thought he would notice.

'I know you've got legs, but you seem determined to keep them hidden. Don't you ever wear dresses?'

'Not very often,' she responded. 'They simply aren't practical in the studio, and anyway I loathe tights.'

'What about the evenings?' he pressed. 'Dinners, dances, that sort of thing.'

She shrugged. 'Not my scene.'

'You can't dance?' He sounded surprised.

'I never said that. As a matter of fact, I love dancing. Its just—well, I don't get much time or opportunity to think about socialising.'

He pulled the car to a halt outside a small barn, newly converted into a double garage, and separated from the cottage garden by a thick hedge. Half turning in his seat, he looked at her for a moment, his voice gently chiding. 'You know what they say about all work and no play.'

'Yes,' Kersty retorted drily. 'Given a little luck, you get to be pretty successful. Only in my case it didn't quite work out.' Picking up her bag and the tape recorder from beside her feet, she opened the door and got out.

Slamming his own door, Neil came to her side and, taking her elbow, guided her through the gap in the hedge, and up the path to the cottage door. 'What do you mean, it didn't work out?' Putting the key back in his trouser pocket, he stood back and gestured for Kersty to go in. 'How many commissions can you handle at once? Isn't this enough to be going on with?'

He closed the door, leaning against it as she looked at him, all the doubt and uncertainty that had been gnawing away beneath her excitement suddenly visible on her face.

'I know you're good,' he teased. 'After all, you did come highly recommended. But even you can only do so much in a day.'

'I've still got the job, then?' Her voice was a mixture of hope and incredulity.

He frowned. Pushing himself upright, he took off his jacket and slung it across the back of the sofa. His tie followed. 'I don't understand.'

'Well,' she moved uncomfortably, 'I made such a hash of the interview. I didn't even manage one question before the TV people took over. You were obviously furious, then Miles guessed I didn't have a contract with you——' She broke off, flinching at his expression.

'You had my word.' His tone was icy. 'Isn't that good enough?'

Kersty swallowed. *Oh, God, what had she done?* 'Y-yes, I know,' she stammered, 'but——'

'But you prefer the security of a written contract, so that if I renege on the agreement, which you clearly expect me to do, you'll have something to produce in court when you sue me.'

'No—yes! Look,' she cried, 'that wasn't what I meant——'

'Really?' His sarcasm was biting. 'That's exactly what it sounded like to me.'

Kersty's anger bubbled up and boiled over. 'Listen, my business nearly went broke because I trusted people. Maybe I've done you an injustice. If so, I apologise. But don't get high-handed with me because I want to protect something I've worked damned hard for.' She could feel herself shaking. 'You *must* know that without a written contract neither of us is legally bound. You could have changed your mind this afternoon and given the job to...to someone else.' She could not bring herself to mention Miles Quintrell's name. 'I hope you won't. I want to do it, very much.' Chin high, heart pounding, she met his gaze squarely. 'But if I'm to continue working for you, you'll have to show a little more understanding of my feelings and be less wrapped up in your own.' Her face was on fire and she felt almost sick with trepidation. But it had needed saying.

'I see.' He bit the words off. His eyes were shadowed, his expression unreadable. 'It didn't occur to you, I suppose, that the reason I looked furious had nothing to do with your attack of nerves which, under the circumstances was perfectly understandable, and everything to do with that obnoxious young TV reporter's pushing you aside?' Kersty's eyes widened. 'And that my sole purpose in hearing out Miles Quintrell's sales spiel was to see if there was any aspect concerning this project that might have been overlooked.' He paused. 'As it happens, there was.'

'Oh,' Kersty whispered. She lowered her head for a moment, hearing her own words echo, loud and mocking, in her ears. She had accused *him* of being immersed in his own feelings. *What about herself?*

'What can I say?' she whispered. Clutching her bag, she twisted the strap between her fingers. 'On the phone, you said...you said this was a new experience for you.'

'It is,' he agreed quietly.

She glanced up, meeting his gaze, and took a deep breath. 'I'm not referring to the project.'

'Nor was I,' he said.

'But you do know I want to make a success of it, a really big success? Not just because of the money, though obviously that is important.' She grinned shakily. 'Important? Who am I kidding? Without it I'm wiped out.' She was immediately serious again, desperately wanting him to understand. 'Well, I want to justify your faith in me.'

He would have spoken then, but she lifted her hand quickly to stop him. He caught it in one of his. 'Go on,' he ordered tersely.

She moistened dry lips. 'But, as there *is* more than just work involved here, I—you——' She shrugged helplessly and stared at her feet.

'Kersty?' He waited until she looked up, then, as their eyes met, he raised her hand to his mouth and pressed his lips to her open palm, then held it against his cheek.

His skin was warm, firm along his jaw, and rough with faint beard stubble.

'What are you afraid of? The past? Me? The differences between us?'

She shook her head, though doubt clouded her face. 'Not you, not the man I met in the woods, though the other will take a little longer to get used to. No, it's—I—it's just——'

'It's all happened rather quickly?' His voice was gentle and she sensed the underlying note of laughter was directed against himself and not at her.

She bit her lip. 'That's part of it.'

'And the rest?' he prompted, bringing her hand to his lips once more and pressing tiny kisses to the flesh at the base of her thumb.

'Well, I—I'm not...' *beautiful, or sophisticated, I don't know how to tease and flirt, I've been hurt and I'm not hard enough not to care. I think I'm falling in love with you and I'm scared—no, I'm terrified* ' . . . not the kind of girl you're used to.'

'No,' he agreed. Swiftly, her eyes searched his, and found only tenderness.

She shrugged, and tried to smile.

'No,' he repeated softly. 'I've never met anyone quite like you,' he paused. Gently taking the tape recorder and bag from her unresisting hands, he placed them on the nearest chair. Straightening up, he rested his hands on the curve between her neck and shoulder. She had to tilt her head back to meet his gaze. 'You're independent, impulsive, prickly, vulnerable, funny, warm, and very. . .' he lowered he head towards hers 'very. . .' his voice dropped to a hoarse murmur, 'special.'

His mouth was warm and caressing, and after a moment's shy hesitation Kersty gave herself up to the delicious sensation of his lips parting hers and the tip of his tongue gently exploring the inner softness of her mouth.

He drew her closer. One hand buried itself in her hair, dislodging her scarf so it fell in a tiny silken pool to the floor. The other traced her spine, making her quiver and gasp as, involuntarily, she arched against him.

His body quickened and she heard his whispered intake of breath, then a soft, incoherent sound deep in his throat as his fingers spread at the base of her spine, melding her to him.

Crushed against the hard wall of his chest, her breasts hurt, but it was a deeply pleasurable ache, unlike anything she had ever experienced before, and she welcomed it. She could smell the subtle fragrance of his aftershave, feel his body heat and the rhythmic thud of his heart. Every sense was finely tuned to a new level of awareness. Her hands explored his shoulders, feeling the curves and ridges of muscle through his shirt, slid to the strong column of his neck, and up into the thick hair that curled just above his collar. Nothing existed but this moment and the powerful emotions binding them.

When at last they drew apart, Kersty could not speak. Breathless and trembling, she was perilously near to tears.

Holding her close, Neil stroked her hair. 'It's all right,' he whispered.

She nodded, clinging to him. 'I just didn't expect...I've never felt...'

Gently tilting her chin, he looked deep into her eyes. And smiled, 'What would you say to a cup of tea, then a long talk?'

Eyes shining, face aglow, she grinned tremulously. 'I thought you'd never ask.'

CHAPTER SIX

THE TREES cast long shadows, their fresh young leaves illuminated by slanting golden beams as Neil and Kersty walked, hand in hand, past the sea of bluebells to the white gate.

It was almost six-thirty. The drone of chainsaws and the throaty roar of tractor and mechanical digger had long ceased. Workmen busy in the converted out-buildings had left for home an hour before. Apart from the household staff and gardeners, now at their tea, there was no one left on the estate but themselves.

The trees whispered and sighed. High overhead a lone seagull soared, its mournful cry snatched away by the breeze.

Carrying the tape recorder by its strap, her bag tucked in the crook of her arm, Kersty glanced down at the thick sweater reaching mid-way to her knees, and smiled.

Neil had offered her the choice of a lift back to the Flower Festival, or a walk through the woods to the estate's lower entrance, a padlocked gate festooned with barbed wire at the end of a lane off the village's main street. When she chose the walk, he had fetched the sweater, insisting she wear it against the evening chill.

Now she was glad of it. The thick wool was warm over her silk shirt, and smelled of him, a faint, musky fragrance.

How they talked! For over three hours, until their throats were parched and the dregs of the second pot of tea stone-cold.

At first she had been hesitant, acutely aware that, despite the powerful attraction between them, they had known each other barely a week. But as Neil probed, teased and coaxed, her diffidence evaporated, burned away by her fascination with him.

He spoke of his two sisters, one married to a breeder of polo-ponies and living in Argentina, the other an Australian rancher's wife, and of his five nephews and nieces. He told her more about his work in Brazil. She recalled his brief reference to a death in the family being one of the reasons for his return to England. Tentatively, she had asked about it.

After a moment's silence he told her how the light plane, piloted by his father, and carrying his fiancée who had arrived that day for two weeks' holiday, had crashed into the forest. Neil himself had led the rescue party. They had searched for three days and nights before finding what was left of the bodies.

Shaken, Kersty had fought back tears as she listened to the story. She had no right to cry. It was his tragedy, not hers. If he could handle it with such quiet dignity, then so must she. But, having known the pain of loss herself, her heart bled for him.

No wonder she had sensed deeper, darker currents. But the totally feminine side of her nature could not help wondering if he still grieved for the woman he had lost. If the flame of memory still burned brightly, might she not be eclipsed by it?

She had pushed the thought away, unwilling to accept the possibility, refusing to acknowledge just how much it mattered.

She had told him about her mother's illness and its effect on the family. And, for only the second time in her life, recounted the way Martin had jilted her. Her voice was calm and factual as she described her father's insistence she pretend everything was fine to spare her mother further distress.

To her surprise, telling Neil had not been the ordeal she had anticipated. Distanced by time, and by the powerful feelings he had aroused in her, she found herself able to think of the whole episode almost as if it had happened to someone else. Perhaps, in a way, it had. For she was no longer the same person.

Neil's lips pressed to her temple, and the tightening of his arms around her in long-denied comfort soothed and healed.

Now, as they left the park and followed the path through the woods, a thick carpet of leaf-mould deadening their footsteps, excitement simmered in Kersty. As she learned more about the man beside her, she was discovering someone else, a stranger, *herself*.

'Kersty——' Neil broke into her thoughts and she turned her head to look at him. The upturned collar of the battered brown leather flying-jacket he had pulled on over his open-necked white shirt angled down his cheekbone, giving him a faintly piratical air. 'There's no easy way of saying this. Please try to understand.'

Her stomach contracted. The words were ominous. So was the silence, as he visibly searched for the right way of putting across what was on his mind. Her mind raced as dread slid cold tentacles around her heart. *She should have known it was all too good to be true.*

Her hand slackened on his. Already she was withdrawing, steeling herself in automatic self-protection as she prepared for the blow.

What was she doing? She had already jumped to one wrong conclusion about his reactions in the marquee, and was in grave danger of repeating the mistake. What was the worst he could say? That he didn't want to see her again?

But that wasn't possible. Not after today. Not after the kisses that had stirred them both so deeply. Not after the way they had talked, confiding thoughts and experiences never before shared with a living soul. It *couldn't* be that.

He stopped walking and, raising her hand, lightly kissed her knuckles. She waited, hardly daring to breathe.

'There are going to be problems, Kersty. The kind of problems ordinary people aren't usually called upon to face.'

'Are we that special?'

His smile held a trace of cynicism. 'Unfortunately, yes. Look,' his voice was gentle, 'I wasn't exaggerating about the dangers of premature publicity. It *must* be avoided. At least until we've had more time, and you are a lot more certain about your feelings about...' he broke off, then made a brief gesture, 'about all of this.'

'Oh, Neil,' she began, a flood of words ready to tumble out in her happiness and relief. 'I don't need t——'

He placed his fingertips on her mouth, effectively silencing her. 'Let me finish, please?'

She nodded. He was worrying about nothing. She knew how she felt. It wouldn't be easy to tell him. For one thing she had never before experienced such exhilaration, such strange, trembly excitement. But time wasn't going to change that. In any case, she certainly didn't need any more time to convince her that meeting him was the most important event in her life, and that the more she learned about him, and the more time they spent together, the more powerful and binding the attraction became.

He touched her face, a gesture of tenderness acknowledging her willingness to listen and silently thanking her for it. Drawing her hand through his arm, he covered it with his own, and they started walking again.

'The fact that I have commissioned you to design the brochures and make a promotional video for Ravenswood will not pass unremarked. You are a very...' his voice softened to match his smile '... *very* attractive woman.'

Kersty blushed with pleasure and darted a sidelong grin at him. 'You're a cut above the average yourself.'

Irony lifted one corner of his mouth. 'Believe me, it wouldn't make any difference if I looked like the hunchback of Notre-Dame.'

A puzzled frown creased Kersty's forehead. 'Of course it would, I mean, I know looks aren't everything, personality counts...'

He shook his head. 'You're missing the point. What I'm saying is that we are likely to be the target of a lot of gossip and innuendo. Which is one of the reasons I feel it would be best if the personal aspect of our relationship is kept totally secret. You must not tell *anyone*. Not even your family. And certainly not your friends.'

From the bitter disgust edging his tone, Kersty guessed that in the past some girl or her *friends* had bought fleeting fame at his expense.

Her brow furrowed. 'I'm not sure I understand. If we're—working together, well, surely that's a perfectly legitimate reason for us to be seen together?' A battle was raging inside her. On one hand, she could see the logic of keeping their personal relationship a private matter. After all, it was no one else's business. But the kind of secrecy Neil was insisting on... She couldn't smother a growing unease.

'Oh, Kersty,' he sighed. 'What does it take to get through to you? What exactly do you think some enterprising reporter would make of us wining and dining and dancing together? And you answering his questions with, "I'm working for Viscount Haldane, that's all. We're just good friends." The next question would be, "What kind of work?" And then, "How come a tiny company like yours got the job?" And, "Isn't it true you were in severe financial difficulties?" And, "What can you offer his Lordship that a large, long-established company like Duchy Design can't? *As if we didn't know.*"'

Kersty paled. 'No.' She shook her head, horrified. 'No, that's *awful.*'

Neil's mouth twisted. 'That's just for starters.'

Kersty stared, unseeing, at the path, trying to come to terms with what he was telling her. 'But...but why should the Press even know if we went out to dinner, or...dancing?'

Neil's face was stony. 'They'd be tipped off. Newspapers thrive on whispers. Not all their informants do it for money. Some work on a favour-for-favour basis. Others consider it,' his sarcasm was biting, 'a public duty. And with some it's just spite. In which category would you place Miles Quintrell?'

Kersty's eyes widened and her head flew up. *'Miles?'*

'You sound surprised,' Neil observed drily. 'You shouldn't. Your refusal to sell really hit him where it hurt—in his ego. Added to which, you obtained a commission he considered should have been offered to his company.'

'But I turned down his offer *before* we—*before* anything...' She faltered, her cheeks rosy. 'Did he say something about all this in the marquee?'

Neil squeezed her hand gently. 'He said a lot of things, most of which are best forgotten. But the point is that he, or someone like him, could cause us a lot of unpleasantness.'

'So,' her tone was hollow, matching the sudden emptiness yawning inside her, 'you do want us to be furtive...'

Releasing her hand, he seized her shoulders, pulling her round to face him. His thin face was dark with anger and his eyes had a steely glitter. 'You see how it starts? The doubts? The misunderstanding?' He made a visible effort to control himself. 'That's not what I want at all.' He was brusque. 'I thought I'd made it clear. My concern is for *you*. I want to come to the studio, and I want you to come to Ravenswood. In fact, you have to, to film the house and grounds. But we will be meeting in a professional capacity and must behave accordingly. Surely that's not unreasonable?'

'No,' she admitted.

'Look at me,' he commanded.

Slowly she raised her eyes.

'Kersty, we are both involved in work we care deeply about. Though it wasn't directly responsible for our first meeting,' he paused, his mouth twitching in a fleeting smile, 'it has brought us together.'

The foreboding that had drawn her nerves wire-taut began to lift.

'We have a unique opportunity to learn about each other's working life,' he went on, 'about the pressures and problems as well as the satisfactions. Kersty, don't you see?' He shook her gently. 'Ravenswood was your childhood. It's my future. All this——' he flung his arm wide, encompassing not only the woods, but the park and house '—is part of us both. It's not a barrier, it's a bond.'

His hand fastened on her shoulder once more, his fingers gripping, unwittingly hurting her in his desire to make her understand. 'We are on the threshold of something very, very special. But we must be patient.'

He held her gaze for a moment longer, then pulled her roughly to him. The sudden shock of his body against hers took Kersty's breath away.

One arm encircled her waist. His other hand buried itself in her hair as he laid his cheek against her temple. 'How glibly I talk of patience.' Kersty winced at his blistering self-mockery. '*Patience* is the last thing I feel when I'm with you. I want you to remember that when I seem distant. God knows, it's not because I don't want to be close to you, to touch, to hold you like this, to kiss you, and explore that beautiful, mysterious body.'

Kersty closed her eyes as his husky voice sent shivers of delight along her limbs.

'It would be all too easy to throw caution to the winds, to take you to all the best restaurants, and show you off. But if, in a few weeks' time, either of us decided that the relationship wasn't working out, it's *you* who'd be caught in the backlash, *your* name and reputation the village gossips would tear to shreds.' He rubbed his cheek against her hair. 'Tell me I'm wrong,' he demanded softly.

Kersty drew back. Meeting his gaze, she shrugged in painful recognition of the truth. 'No,' she admitted, 'you're quite right.'

She could hear them already, Aggie Collins, Flo Hosking and Marge Tallack. The black widows, they were dubbed by the rest of the village. Related by marriage and living side by side in a terrace of cob-walled cottages, they were named partly for their status, all three husbands having embraced eternal peace many years previously, and partly for their habit of weaving webs of suspicion and half-truth, laced with the acid of frustration and spite that masqueraded as high moral tone.

They would make it their business to tell everyone who would listen how they'd known all along it would never work, that she was no better than she should be, throwing herself at him like that, that she'd been asking for trouble and would pay for her folly. The heads would nod, the tongues would click, and if she appeared in the village in anything loose-fitting, their stares would focus on her waistline.

The imagined comments echoed loud in her head, and her father's doubts returned, adding to the cacophony. Neil was an aristocrat, a much-travelled man of the world.

Though intelligent, independent and capable, she was still only a village girl. There was no denying the flaring physical attraction between them, but what hope was there of a long-term future?

Even as the thought formed, she was overwhelmed by the realisation that her unconscious mind had already begun to think in terms of a *lifetime*.

She lowered her head, but not quickly enough, for Neil seized her face in his hands.

'Don't,' he grated. 'Please, darling, don't look like that.' He rained tiny kisses on to her temple, her eyelids, her cheek, and finally, her mouth.

'Trust me,' he murmured against her lips. 'Kersty, you need time and space to be sure of what you feel. I intend to make sure you get both. Will you trust me?'

Eyes bright with unshed tears, she looked up at him. Everything was far more complicated than she had ever imagined it would be. That was not his fault, it was just the way things were. She swallowed and tried to smile. 'I don't have much choice, do I?' *She was more than half in love with him already.*

He did not return her smile. 'There's always a choice,' he said quietly. 'You are free to turn me down, to walk away.'

Free? The word bubbled up hysterically inside her. She was as free to stop breathing.

'But,' he added, tension audible in his voice, 'If that's what you intend to do, for pity's sake, do it now while I'm still capable of pretending it doesn't matter.'

'Oh, Neil,' she whispered and clung to him, burying her face in the warm curve of his neck and shoulder as his arms fastened round her, lifting her off the ground. 'I do understand, and I'm sure you're right, but...'

He held her away from him, searching her face. 'But?'

'Well...if we're to be so circumspect during business hours, and not be seen together in public afterwards, when *can* we behave like ordinary people? And where?'

His eyes burned with a hunger, a yearning, that sent a delicious spasm of shock knifing through her, and her heart gave an almost painful kick.

'The cottage is my home, my retreat, the place where I can forget all the pressures and responsibilities. No one outside the estate knows I live there. The staff, and Mrs Laity, are sworn to secrecy. Will you come to me there, Kersty? There'll be no looking over our shoulders, no hiding or pretence. We will be free and quite alone.' His voice roughened. 'Will you come? Soon?'

She hesitated, but only for a moment. Then all her uncertainty dissolved, replaced by serene happiness. She smiled up at him. 'I'd like that.'

His lean, hard-muscled body was taut, unyielding, and as he tilted her head to take possession of her lips a tremor shook him.

She expected fierceness, a passion to match that in his eyes. But his mouth was gentle, caressing hers with a sweet sensuality that sent sudden heat coursing through her veins.

After what seemed like a lifetime, he raised his head. Her legs felt boneless. Slowly she opened her eyes, only to be hypnotised by the rhythmic pulse beneath the skin on one side of his throat. She had never thought of him as vulnerable, yet that pulse...

'I think,' his voice was husky and seemed to come from far away, 'we'd better go.'

'Yes,' she murmured, but did not, could not, move.

His body stirred against hers and she caught her breath.

'Kersty...' The strain in his voice pierced her languor, bringing her sharply back to reality, and to awareness of his battle for control.

A blush bloomed on her cheeks. She took a small, stumbling step backwards, still caught within the circle of his arms. There was an indefinable ache where, only moments before, the lower half of Neil's body, so closely moulded to hers, had generated voluptuous warmth.

'I...I'm sorry, I...'

'Ssshh!' He kissed her forehead. 'An apology's the last thing I want. Mind you,' he grimaced wryly, 'abstinence was never a problem,' he paused, 'until you came into my life.'

At his words, her confidence in herself as a woman, so fragile since Martin's defection, took off like a rocket. She slanted him a teasing smile from beneath her lashes. 'Is that so?'

Neil seemed momentarily taken aback, then he closed his eyes and groaned. 'Oh, lord, what *have* I done?' Opening one eye, he grinned and hugged her close.

His arm rested on her shoulders and hers was around his waist as they followed the curving path past a clump of rhododendron bushes. About twenty yards ahead, bound with barbed wire which stretched three strands deep along the top of a moss-covered stone hedge, was the gate and, beyond it, the lane leading down to the village.

They exchanged a brief glance. Neil's arm tightened momentarily, and reluctance to leave him slowed Kersty's footsteps.

They stopped, and by unspoken agreement moved slightly apart, turning to face one another.

'So,' he said softly, 'when shall I see you again?'

She clutched the tape recorder and her bag, desperate to find something to do with hands that longed to stroke his face or touch the thick hair that was dark underneath and streaked with gold where the sun had lightened it. 'Soon?' she pleaded. 'Though you did say you would be very busy all this week.'

He nodded. 'Among other things, I'm interviewing prospective staff for the hotel. I need a first-class housekeeper, senior receptionist and chef. Thank God I don't need to worry about getting a manager as well. George is admirably suited for that position. But the success of the venture will depend on them.'

Kersty was shaken. 'You're not going to run it yourself?' She recalled her father's warning that Neil would install a manager, *then move on*.

He shook his head. 'No. I've enjoyed setting it all up, despite the problems. That was the real challenge. Naturally, I'll keep an eye on things, but the day-to-day running doesn't interest me. With the right staff, George could run the hotel with one hand tied behind him.' He looked around. 'This is where I want to be.'

As he gazed up at the oak and and chestnut trees, his voice became reflective.

'In Brazil the temperature rarely dropped below seventy-eight degrees, and the humidity made even breathing an effort sometimes. The trees were giants: Para chestnut, Brazilian rosewood and mahogany. Instead of thrushes and robins we had humming-birds and, down by the river, flamingoes and egrets. There were butterflies as big as my hand and ants that marched in armies. Instead of foxes, badgers and rabbits, we had monkeys, wild boar and jaguars. It was a vivid, primaeval place. But this,' he turned his gaze on her and she saw enthusiasm burning brightly in his eyes, 'this is home.'

But for how long? Kersty wondered.

'I have a thousand acres of woodland here,' Neil said, 'much of it still badly neglected. A wood isn't just a bunch of trees. It's a living thing, with an eco-system all its own. Like all living things, it needs tending. The old, diseased trees must be culled and new ones planted. Not impenetrable rows of conifers that deface the countryside and kill off the wildlife, but oak, willow, ash, beech and elm. Undergrowth must be cleared, drainage ditches maintained and nurseries established for seedlings and saplings.'

'It sounds as if it could be rather a big job,' Kersty observed lightly. 'Do you plan to do it all by yourself?'

Her knuckles gleamed as she waited for his reply. *How long?*

Turning his head slowly, Neil scanned the area, a satisfied smile lifting the corners of his mouth. 'Hardly. But I'm only taking on men who genuinely love the work. I have two already, and we get along well. Of course, if I get involved, as I hope to, on the business side of the craft units, setting up outlets both in this country and abroad, I rather think I'll have more than enough to keep me busy for the rest of my life.'

Kersty relaxed, letting her breath out gradually. She had her answer from Neil's own lips. He was here to stay.

'You did say you'd like to come and look around the studio,' she ventured. 'But it sounds as though...'

He didn't wait for her to finish. 'Just try to keep me away.'

She pretended to give his remark serious consideration, then shook her head. 'No, you're bigger than me.' She thought for a moment, then looked up at him. 'If I really press on, I could have a mock-up of the brochure ready, plus a rough storyboard. You'd be able to see how we plan to put the film together.'

'I'm really looking forward to this.' His voice caressed her, warm and admiring. 'You, Kersty Hurrell, are a woman of many talents. And I am finding all of them quite fascinating.'

Aware from the undertone of mild surprise that his remark was heartfelt and not mere flattery, Kersty glowed with pleasure.

'In the meantime,' he went on, 'how much experience do you have in marketing?'

She shook her head. 'Very little. It has become such a complex and wide-ranging business, not to mention time-consuming, that...' She broke off, her hand flying to her mouth as comprehension dawned. 'Was *that* what Miles...yes, of course... Oh, lord, that's something I should have thought of. But normally I only handle design. The client either does his own marketing, or employs a company of his own choice.'

'Stop panicking,' he chided gently. 'I don't think a locally based company would have the scope or weight we need. We're aiming at the top end of the market,' he pointed out. 'People with not only the money, but the perception to understand and appreciate what Ravenswood has to offer. Look, leave it to me. There's a company I know of in London. I think they'll be exactly what we need. Is it all right with you if I drop them a line?'

'Of course.' Kersty heaved a sigh of relief. 'Thank heaven for your contacts. That side of it is rather outside my experience.'

He laid one hand on her shoulder, his fingers firm and warm through the thick wool. 'Leave it to me. You already have more than enough to handle on the creative side. Look, don't think I'm rushing you—I want the best possible job, and I know that takes time—but roughly how long will it be before we have something to show the marketing people?'

Kersty did some rapid mental calculations. 'At the earliest, I'd say two weeks. I can probably get the brochure finished by next Monday or Tuesday. But the printers will take a week or possibly longer. Still, there's nothing to stop you contacting the company before. In fact, it might be a good idea. At least we'd know in advance how many brochures and copies of the video they'll want, and what type of advertising and distribution they have in mind. As for the video itself, I'd like to start filming the interiors on Monday. Depending on the weather, the outside shots—the gardens, any specially atmospheric locations, plus the aerial views—could be completed by the following weekend. Would that be all right?'

His smile lit up his eyes, deepening the creases at their corners. 'It's a real pleasure doing business with such a professional.'

Kersty inclined her head. 'Well, thank you, sir. We aim to please.'

His grip on her shoulder tightened and he drew her forward. 'You do that all right,' he agreed softly. 'You please me very much. You also... tantalise...' His voice faded to silence as his eyes roamed her face as if committing it to memory.

Eyes wide, lips parted, she hung in his gaze. How she longed for him to kiss her, just once more. Unconsciously she swayed towards him. The slight movement brought a brief sound that was almost a groan from deep in his throat and, lowering his head, he covered her mouth with his own.

When he straightened up, releasing her shoulder, he shoved his hands into the slit pockets of the flying-jacket. 'Go home, Kersty,' he grated, 'before I forget all my good intentions.'

Laying her bag and tape recorder on the ground, she struggled out of the sweater and handed it to him. 'Thank you. It was lovely and warm.'

Swinging it over his arm, he unlocked the gate and held it open for her, relocking it again as soon as she was on the other side. 'Go on,' he commanded brusquely, 'before you get chilled.'

'Yessir,' she snapped a mocking salute.

His eyes narrowed. 'I'll see you on Friday.'

Excitement fizzed along her veins at the threat and promise in his voice. Raising her hand in silent farewell, Kersty walked quickly down the lane. She looked back once. Neil still stood behind the gate. He had the sweater to his face, and a smile curved her mouth as she realised he was inhaling the faint trace of her perfume.

As she walked in through the kitchen door, three faces turned to greet her. Sue, Josh and her father were all seated at the kitchen table with the remains of their evening meal in front of them.

'Hi. Where did you get to?' Josh helped himself to another slice of cake.

'I...went for a walk,' Kersty answered carefully. She wasn't going to lie if she could possibly avoid it. Placing her bag and recorder on the dresser, she went to the sink and washed her hands, needing time to gather her wits and prepare herself for possible questions.

'Are you all right, love?' Her father's face was sympathetic. 'Josh tells me you had a rather difficult time.'

'That creep, Quintrell,' Sue muttered. 'I don't usually ill-wish people, but I wouldn't grieve if he got what was owing to him.'

'What did you all have?' Kersty asked, indicating the plates, anxious to steer the conversation on to safer ground.

'Bacon, egg, sausage and tomato,' Josh replied. 'Sue cooked for us, as you weren't here.'

'You really are the limit,' Kersty scolded, but her tone held more resignation than anger. 'You are perfectly capable of cooking a meal yourself. So's Dad, for that matter.' She looked at her father, who was suddenly busy tamping and re-lighting his pipe.

'Sue likes doing it. She's getting some practice in. Isn't that right, love?'

Her back to Josh, Sue rolled her eyes at Kersty. 'One of these days I'll say no. Then where will you be, Josh Hurrell?' She leaned over to pour them all a second cup of tea.

'Hungry.' Josh grinned, sliding an arm around her waist as she stopped beside his chair.

Sue ruffled his hair. You're hopeless.'

He winked at her. 'But ever so lovable.'

Sue glanced round at Kersty, who had the fridge door open. 'So what did his Lordship want?'

Kersty almost dropped the tray of eggs. 'I beg your pardon?'

Putting the teapot down, Sue resumed her seat and picked up her cup. 'It was him you were talking to, wasn't it? Over between the tea-tent and the car park.'

Kersty shut the door with her foot and took the eggs to the worktop next to the cooker. 'Yes. I—I was apologising for messing up the interview. He was charming about it. Said it could have happened to anyone.' She reached into the cupboard for a glass bowl and took a fork from the cutlery drawer in the dresser.

'What about Quintrell?' Josh demanded. 'Did his Lordship say anything about him? Or what they'd been talking about?'

'Josh!' Sue broke in. 'You couldn't have expected him to.'

'He was quite angry.' Kersty broke two eggs into the bowl, added salt, pepper and a little water, and began beating the mixture with a fork. 'His Lordship, I mean. As far as he's concerned, his word is as binding as any contract, and he was furious that I could even think he'd consider changing horses in mid-stream, so to speak. The job is still ours.'

Sue and Josh both let out loud sighs of relief.

'Then what?' Josh pressed.

Kersty shrugged. 'Then he went home.'

She turned away to wipe the frying pan out, gripping the handle tightly to cover the tremor in her hand as Josh said sympathetically, 'I bet you were glad to see the back of him. Enough's enough for one day.'

CHAPTER SEVEN

DURING the next two days Kersty worked harder than she ever had in her life. She was at the studio by eight-thirty a.m. and didn't leave until almost ten in the evening. Her lunch break was a mere half-hour, and the cup of coffee and snack that served as her tea were swallowed while she checked and signed the day's post.

The occasional nagging pains beneath her breastbone bothered her a little, but she forced herself to ignore them, blaming the discomfort on long hours spent at the drawing-board and meals eaten too quickly. In any case, she was far too happy and busy to fret about a touch of indigestion.

Since meeting Neil, everything in her life had taken a turn for the better. Yesterday the cheque had arrived from the Tourist Board, and this morning she had taken on another designer. From teetering on the edge of destruction, the company had taken a great leap into healthy new life.

Dena Graham had trained in London but, following the birth of her son, had been out of the business for almost five years. She had only recently moved into the area, her husband's company appointing him to open a new branch in the town. As their little boy had just started school, Dena was keen to resume her career, though on a part-time basis only.

She had called at the studio on impulse while shopping, just as Sue managed to persuade Kersty to stop for coffee and a breather.

As far as Kersty was concerned, Dena was a gift from heaven. She could not really justify or afford to take anyone on full-time, so Dena's swift and delighted acceptance of three hours each morning, Monday to Friday, provided the ideal solution.

Thus Kersty was spared the hassle of advertising for, and interviewing another designer. It also meant she could tell Sue to accept several offers of work they would otherwise have been forced to turn down.

So, with one less problem to contend with, and Josh, Sue and Harry all fully occupied with their own work, she was able to devote her total attention to Neil's project.

It was coming together beautifully. She had prepared mock-ups of two brochures. Both were approximately eleven inches high, eight inches wide, and contained four pages. One was a heavyweight, thickly textured paper the colour of clotted cream, with fine purple borders surrounding the sketches which represented the photographs yet to be taken, and a mixture of Roman and Italic typeface.

The other was of thick, glossy pine-green paper. The photographs were to be mounted on white borders outlined with a narrow red band. The bold Century Textbook typeface was crisp and clear-cut.

The mock-ups completed and put carefully aside to await Neil's approval and final choice, she began work on the storyboard.

She knew from their conversations the image Neil wanted to present in the video, and raked over her own memories of the place for features deserving special attention, incorporating both into the plan.

Sue and Josh left at six, and Kersty waited until they had gone before sitting back from her drawing-board. Excitement had begun to seethe inside, making her feel slightly queasy, and she had been terrified of betraying herself. But with Harry shut in the editing-room, she could allow herself a few moments to stop and look forward to seeing Neil. How soon would he come? An hour? Two?

Putting the kettle on, she made some fresh coffee, then took the opportunity to freshen up, retouching her lipstick and pulling her hair loose from its ponytail. After brushing it till it shone and crackled, she fastened it back from her face with a large tortoiseshell clip. Then she drank her coffee and waited.

Six-thirty came, and went. At seven o'clock he still hadn't arrived. Seeking reassurance in the certainty that had he not been able to come he would have let her know, she reminded herself of all the demands on his time, any of which could have delayed him.

Rinsing her coffee-mug, and her mouth, she returned to work and was soon utterly absorbed.

At the sound of the door opening she glanced up, her heart leaping as he strode in. Wearing jeans and a Norwegian-style fisherman's sweater over a warm shirt, his hair wind-blown and his eyes startlingly blue in his tanned face, he looked the ultimate outdoor man.

'Sorry I'm a little late.' His apologetic smile sent a delicious shiver down her spine. How different this was from the last time he had been in the studio. 'It's been one of those days. Anything that could go wrong did, and I was required in six different places at once to make instant decisions.'

'Aaah!' She shook her head, mocking him gently. 'The problems of being a wealthy landowner.' Her shining eyes betrayed her joy at seeing him again.

'A little more respect from the ranks, if you please,' he demanded, adding softly, 'You look very beautiful tonight. I've missed you.'

Kersty could hardly contain her happiness. Climbing down off her stool, she advanced towards him, extending her hand. 'Good evening, My Lord, may I welcome you to K. Graphics.'

His eyes narrowed and a smile flickered across his mouth. Then he assumed his most arrogant expression. 'You may,' he drawled.

As their hands touched, his cool, hers warm, the contact electrifying, the door between the studio and editing-room opened and Harry emerged.

Acknowledging Neil with a murmured, 'Evening,' he turned to Kersty, who hoped fervently her cheeks did not look as red as they felt. She had dropped Neil's hand like a hot potato and had been rewarded by a look brimming with irony.

'I'm just going up home for a bite of supper and to get some bits from my workshop,' Harry announced. 'Then I'll come back and finish off.'

'Are you sure you want to bother, Harry?' Kersty sounded doubtful. 'You've already worked late two nights this week. Wouldn't you rather finish it in the morning?'

'Can't do that, my bird.' He shook his head. 'Joshua is in the middle of editing that there film of the Flower Festival.' He paused, darting a sidelong glance at Neil, then lowered his voice. 'Not in your way, am I?'

'Of course not,' Kersty answered hastily, clasping her hands in front of her. 'My Lord, may I present Harry Hooper, our maintenance engineer and resident miracle worker.'

Harry's eyebrows lifted as he looked from Kersty to the tall man beside her. 'Harry, this is Viscount Haldane.'

'Good evening, Mr Hooper,' Neil held out his hand.

'Call me Harry, sir, everyone does.' After shaking hands, he went on, 'Nice place you've got up there.'

Kersty didn't dare look at Neil as he replied, 'Thank you. It's coming on.'

Turning to her, Harry asked, 'Will you still be here, or shall I take the key?'

'I'll still be here,' she promised.

'Right. I'll see you later, then. You'll—er—be all right on your own?'

'I'm not on my own,' she reminded him, keeping her face straight with great difficulty. 'Viscount Haldane will be here for a while. He wants to see over the studio and as we're so busy during the day, he very kindly agreed to come after office hours.'

'Ah!' Harry stretched his chin. 'Well. Mind you don't touch the console. I haven't finished connecting up.' He stumped out into the darkness, closing the door loudly behind him, leaving Neil and Kersty shaking with laughter.

'I could do with someone like him,' Neil said at last.

'Don't get any ideas,' Kersty warned. 'Poachers aren't popular round here.'

Their eyes met and locked, the smiles faded and the yearning was almost tangible.

It was Neil who broke the contact. Hooking his thumbs on to the lower edge of his jeans pockets, he looked around the studio. 'So. Where shall we begin?'

Pushing a stray lock of hair back from her forehead, Kersty half turned away. 'Would you like to see the editing suite?'

He nodded. 'I would.'

Kersty led the way. It was a narrow room, made even narrower by the deep bench running the length of one wall. Two swivel chairs were pushed carelessly aside.

Neil followed her in, not quite touching, but close enough for her to be vividly aware of him. 'Why do you have two tape-decks and two TV screens?' He indicated the equipment separated by the control console, a mass of knobs and dials, one panel of which had been un-screwed and lifted out to reveal a mass of wiring.

'The deck on the left plays back the film from the video camera which shows on the small monitor,' she explained. 'The deck on the right, which is connected to the large screen, holds the master tape on to which the edited film is recorded.'

As he leaned forward to get a closer look at the controls, his chest brushed lightly against her back, setting all her nerve-ends jangling as she moved a little to one side.

'What about sound?' he asked, studying the layout.

'The camera records both sound and film simultaneously.' She clasped her upper arms, pressing them against her midriff to ease the niggling pangs. 'But if you want voice-over or background music, or even to erase certain unwanted sounds, like aeroplane noise, that is done on the master tape after editing. To add music, we use the record deck or cassette player on the far right.'

Neil nodded thoughtfully. 'It looks a very professional set-up. Tell me, who does the voice-over?'

'I've done two myself,' she admitted. 'But for clients who prefer a male voice, we use the leading man from the local amateur dramatic society. He's really very good. He has a clear voice, low-pitched and well modulated but not at all *actor-like*. Have you considered which you would prefer?' She glanced up at him and immediately wished she hadn't, for the urge to touch him, to push back the wind-ruffled hair and trace the outline of his face was almost irresistible.

Something of her thoughts must have shown, for his eyes grew smoky and his features tightened. They looked at one another for a long moment. 'I can't say I have. Perhaps it's a matter for consultation with the marketing people.' He moved fractionally towards her. Then, visibly tense, he muttered, 'I think we'd better go back into the studio.'

She swallowed. 'Yes, of course. Please——' She indicated the door and, as he strode out ahead of her, sucked in a deep, steadying breath.

He sat on the edge of the bench, one foot firmly on the floor, the other swinging gently a few inches above it.

Perched on her stool, Kersty outlined the order of development from the client's initial enquiry to the finished product. The physical distance between them made it easier for her to concentrate.

She watched him carefully as he examined both the brochure mock-ups.

'Which do you prefer?' he asked, looking from one to the other, then glancing up.

'That doesn't matter,' Kersty told him. 'I've tried to approach the design from two different angles.' She grinned. 'I started off with three, but the other one simply didn't work. With the cream and purple, I've aimed for elegance and subtlety, almost understatement. I've tried to convey an atmosphere of peace and unashamed luxury. In the other,' she indicated the green brochure, 'the house still features strongly, but I've made more of the surroundings. *I* think——' She broke off, colouring slightly. 'It's your decision. You know best the kind of people you want to attract, and which aspects will appeal most to them.'

He flicked through both brochures again. 'When will you have the actual photographs?'

'Josh will take them the day we do the interior filming. We'll need special lights, you see.'

Nodding, Neil bent his head. Kersty was content to sit and observe him. It was a joy just to have him here, for once a part of *her* world.

He glanced up, smiling and shaking his head. 'It's not easy. They really are good.'

Her heart turned over at the open admiration in his eyes. 'You needn't sound so surprised,' she teased. 'I did come highly recommended.'

He shot her a hooded glance that spoke volumes. 'This one,' he decided, handing it to her.

Kersty couldn't hide her delight.

'Obviously that was your choice too,' he observed drily.

Her colour deepened. 'It's what *you* want that counts.'

'Well, that's the one. Now, am I right?'

Smiling, she nodded. 'Yes, I hoped you'd choose this one.'

'Why?'

'That,' she pointed to the heavy, textured, cream paper, 'was designed for Viscount Haldane. But this——' she lay the forest-green sheets on her drawing board, smoothing them '—I created this for Neil Drummond.'

Folding his arms, he straightened his legs out in front of him, crossing one ankle over the other. He leaned forward, his expression curious, his gaze intent. 'Explain.' It was a command.

Sudden shyness overwhelmed her. He didn't know it, but he was asking her to lay bare her heart.

Sensing her wariness, his voice softened. 'Please, Kersty. I want to understand.'

'Well,' she began hesitantly, 'the colours, for example. They are all significant. They represent everything I've learned about you, my own fe...observations as well as the things you've told me.' She turned her head away, unable to hold his gaze. 'The dark green is for your beloved woods. The red represents the plants and flowering shrubs. The white bordering the photographs is for your clarity of vision and the bold typeface for your strength of purpose.' Her voice faded and she stared blindly at the edge of her drawing-board.

'Go on.'

She ran her fingertips over the glossy paper. 'I used the same approach in choosing what to put in it. Obviously the house had to be the focal point. But the grounds are much more than just a barrier between it and the local population outside. In the old days, estates like Ravenswood were self-supporting communities. They even used to have their own church. I know there was often an awful lot wrong with the so-called "good old days", but one thing that did exist was a sense of continuity and belonging. People took a pride in craftsmanship, in the creation of something not only functional, but beautiful as well.' She shrugged. 'I know we can't turn the clock back, but there is nothing to stop someone who really cares, someone with the vision and resources, from recalling all that was good about the way of life while relating it to the modern world.'

She raised her eyes to his. 'That's what I tried to convey, the best of both.' Her voice grew stronger and more confident. 'The guests who come to Ravenswood should be aware that it *isn't* simply another luxury hotel, it's part of a way of life. History isn't just the past, it's going on all the time, and they can actually be a part of it. They can watch real craftsmen using tools and methods that have been handed down for generations.'

He stared at her in silence, then drew in a slow, deep breath. 'You really are quite amazing,' he murmured.

Flushed with pleasure and glowing at the wonder in his voice, she made a deprecating gesture. 'All part of the service.'

'I'd say it was rather more than that,' he returned softly. 'In fact——' But he was interrupted by the outer door opening to re-admit Harry.

'Everything all right, then?'

Kersty sensed a certain undercurrent in the apparently casual enquiry. It wasn't quite suspicion, but nor was it mere idle curiosity. She caught Neil's eye and from the glint of suppressed amusement realised that he too was aware of the older man's reservations about evening visits by out-of-the-ordinary clients.

'Perhaps I could have a look at the storyboard?' Neil suggested.

'Yes, of course.'

'Make you both some coffee, shall I?' Harry called from the doorway.

As Kersty looked at Neil, he shook his head. 'Not for me, thanks. I'll have to go soon. I've still a load of paperwork to get through. But, please, you go ahead.'

Wincing slightly, Kersty pressed her fingers just below where her ribcage divided, and shook her head. 'I think I've had too much already.' She swung round on the stool. 'No, thanks, Harry. I'll be calling it a night soon.'

He waved acknowledgment and disappeared into the editing-room.

Neil leaned forward, his voice low, concern drawing his brows together. 'What's the matter? Are you in pain?'

'It's nothing,' she removed her hand quickly from the source of discomfort, making light of it. 'I expect I'm hungry. I've only had a packet of crisps since lunch time.' She didn't think it wise to mention that all she'd eaten for lunch was a tuna fish sandwich and an apple. She knew it wasn't really enough, but hadn't wanted more, not then. But now, unexpectedly, visions of a hot pasty filled her mind, the golden crust cut open to reveal diced potato, onion, swede and succulent chunks of beef, all steaming as the juices dribbled out on to the plate. She wrenched her thoughts away with an almost painful effort.

'Kersty,' Neil was quietly forceful, 'devotion to this project does not require you to starve. You have already justified my faith in you ten times over. You don't have to make yourself ill. In fact, I shall be damned annoyed if you do. I have enough problems already.'

'Who's ill?' She spread her hands. 'For heaven's sake, I missed a meal, that's all.'

'No, that's *not* all. You've missed more than one, by the look of you,' he observed bluntly.

Her eyes sparked a warning. 'Aren't you being rather personal?'

'You bet I am,' he retorted. 'You're a person about whom I happen to care rather a lot.'

'Oh,' she gulped.

'Now, let's have a quick look at the storyboard.'

'Yes, *sir*,' she muttered under her breath as she turned to pick it up.

She didn't hear him move, so his whispered, 'Don't push your luck,' just behind her left ear lifted her right off the stool.

As she whirled round he was once more leaning against the bench, arms folded, his straight brows slightly raised. One look at his expression convinced Kersty not to pursue the matter.

'I—I thought we'd open with aerial views, showing the whole of the estate, then sweep in on a curve to circle the house, and land on the lawn. After some exterior shots of the house, we move inside, show the drawing-room, dining-room and one of the bedrooms, and the views from them, then the leisure facilities. Of course, we will need Redheads for all the interior shots.'

Neil did a double-take. 'You'll need *what*?'

Kersty giggled. 'Don't panic. I'm not suggesting you fill the place with glamour-girls. Redheads are lights, powerful halogen bulbs mounted on a stand. They have adjustable flaps to modify the amount and direction of light so that we can avoid the reflections and shadows which would otherwise spoil the shot. It's all quite scientific.'

'So I'm beginning to realise,' Neil admitted.

'By the way, where *is* the swimming pool?' Kersty asked. 'I bet you didn't get planning permission for it in the main building.'

He grimaced briefly. 'How did you guess? Though, as it happens, it all worked out for the best. The pool and jacuzzi are in the vinery.'

Kersty recalled the huge, airy extension that opened onto the walled garden. As well as the arched windows, the walls and pitched roof were also made of glass, much of it hidden by the wrist-thick vine which had climbed and spread to cover almost the entire inner surface. The last time she had seen it, the shabby paintwork had been cracked and peeling, and the glass covered in green algae, dirt and spider's webs.

'What about the vine?' she asked anxiously.

'It's still going strong. We had the devil's own job protecting it during the alterations. But once the work was complete, all the glass cleaned and the vine properly fastened to the walls and ceiling, it took on a new lease of life. I should think we'll get at least fifty pounds of grapes from it this year.'

'You'll have to start making your own wine,' Kersty said. They looked at one another as the potential of her suggestion took root and blossomed.

'That's not a bad idea,' Neil mused, 'not a bad idea at all. What would you say to another commission?'

Kersty was nonplussed. 'To do what?'

'Design me a label for Ravenswood vintage wine.'

'Ever the businessman,' she taunted.

'Well? Would you do it?'

'Are you serious?'

'Never more so.'

She grinned. 'I'd love to. I've never done one before.'

Neil eased himself off the bench and straightened up. 'I seem to have prompted that reaction rather frequently of late.'

'I'm not complaining,' Kersty said quickly. 'In fact, this commission for you is the most challenging and satisfying work I've ever undertaken. Long may it last.'

The look in his eyes made her feel weak inside. 'Amen to that,' he said softly, and she realised he was referring to far more than just their professional relationship.

The charged silence was broken by the *clunk* of a spanner hitting the floor, followed by Harry's muttered curse.

Kersty's tongue snaked out to moisten her lips. 'Then—er—after filming the pool we'll move on to the rest of the gardens, picking up any special features. That gives you a rough idea of the sequence.'

'Who decides the best angles and so on?'

'Josh does.'

'You're confident he can handle that responsibility?'

Kersty nodded emphatically. 'He has both the talent and the training. And as cameraman, he's the best person to produce the film, though I'm involved with the editing. I'll probably write the script for the voice-over as well, unless your marketing people...' She allowed the suggestion to hang in the air.

'I'm glad you reminded me.' Neil smothered a yawn and stretched. 'They're sending someone down as soon as possible for discussions. Apparently, they think it would be useful to have a marketing strategy worked out *before* the filming is complete. That way any particular feature which might provide a special selling point can be made more of at little or no extra cost.'

She nodded.

'You don't mind?'

She was touched at his concern. 'Of course not.' Kersty linked her hands about her knees. 'It's the sensible, logical thing to do. After all, it's their job to know how best to hook our target audience. That's what you're hiring them for.'

'Right.' He flexed his shoulders. His tone told her he was getting ready to leave. 'So when will you begin filming?'

'Monday morning, weather permitting. The helicopter is arranged for ten a.m.'

'Terrific. I would have liked to come up myself. I haven't seen Ravenswood from the air. But...' He shrugged. Words were unnecessary. The weary movement of his shoulders said more than enough about the pressures and demands on him.

Kersty desperately wanted to prolong his visit, but knew it would be neither fair nor wise. Without waiting for him to make the first move, she got down off her stool and started towards the door. He followed.

The bright lights of the reception area, spilling out through the glass into the darkness, illuminated them as if they were performers on a stage.

They walked together, footsteps slowing and, as they reached the outer door, Neil stopped and turned. He held out his hand and Kersty gripped it. To a casual passer-by the scene would have suggested the departure of someone delighted with the progress of a business deal. And so it was, up to a point.

But no one outside could have guessed, from the polite, almost formal stance of the couple, at the electric atmosphere surrounding them.

Neil's handshake was the first time he had *deliberately* touched her all evening. His firm, warm grasp sent tiny flames licking along Kersty's nerves, and she needed all her strength to resist the magnetic pull of his body.

'I've enjoyed this evening very much.' He still held her hand.

'Me, too.' She studiously avoided his eyes, knowing she would not be able to hide her longing to touch him.

'You obviously have everything well under control.'

The dry irony in his tone brought her head up swiftly. His eyes were ablaze with conflicting emotions, and she realised he was finding this parting every bit as difficult as she was.

She moistened her lips. 'One does one's best.' The words emerged husky with strain.

'Kersty.' Barely audible, his voice was utterly compelling. 'Come and have dinner with me tomorrow night, at the cottage.'

She swallowed, her heart thumping painfully. 'I— thank you, I'd like that.'

His fingers tightened on hers before he let go of her hand. He looked at her intently. 'How will you explain your absence?'

'I hope I won't have to. They're all used to me working late. But if I do, I'll just say I needed a complete break and went to the cinema.'

He nodded. 'Come at seven.' Opening the door, he glanced back at her over his shoulder, winked, and disappeared into the night.

Kersty woke the following morning to grey skies and persistent, heavy rain. But even the foul weather could not dampen her spirits.

After a quick bath, she climbed into her usual jeans and sweatshirt, pushed her feet into comfy trainers and, after brushing her freshly washed hair until it gleamed, twisted it up into a loose knot high on her head.

Standing at her open wardrobe, she studied the contents. Tonight was special. She couldn't go and have dinner with Neil at the cottage wearing *jeans*.

Taking down a dress of peacock-green wool jersey, she lifted the warm fabric. It flowed over her palm like water.

Though she rarely wore dresses, she had been unable to resist this one, bought off the model's back at a fashion show given by an exclusive store for whom she had designed the invitations. Its rich colour and simple, elegant styling had appealed to her artist's eye.

Slipping it off the hanger, she folded it quickly, snatched up her black high heels and put shoes and dress into a carrier bag, adding a slip and an unopened packet of sheer black tights from her dressing-table drawer.

A chunky gold necklace was popped into her shoulder-bag, and she hurried downstairs, especially glad on this particular morning to be the first up.

Placing her breakfast dishes in the sink, hoping they would not still be there when she returned that evening, Kersty picked up the carrier, and her bag, grabbed her beige blouson jacket from the hook in the hall, and hurried out to her car. She always parked on the road, leaving the drive for Josh's van, as he often left lighting equipment in it overnight and the gates could be locked. Their father's old Morris Traveller had first claim on the garage.

As it was a Saturday, there were few phone calls and no visitors. Sue finished typing the contract while Kersty completed the voice-over on the Flower Festival film, reading aloud from the script while Josh timed and recorded.

Josh's shots of the TV company's film and interview had come out perfectly. Seeing Neil on the screen, his crisp white shirt and charcoal suit setting off to perfection his bronzed features, Kersty's heart had turned over, and she had had to look away, gripping her pen tightly to control the sudden tremor in her hands.

Harry had rung just after nine-thirty. As Sue was in the kitchen, Kersty answered the phone.

'What did his Lordship think of it all, then?' Harry asked.

'He was quite impressed,' Kersty rolled her pen over and over in her fingers.

'You never bothered showing anyone around before.'

Acutely aware of his curiosity, Kersty's grip on the phone tightened, but she managed to keep her tone light. 'Let's face it, Harry, we've never had a twenty-thousand pound commission before. You can't really blame the man for wanting to make sure we know what we're doing, and that his money isn't being wasted.'

Reluctantly conceding that she had a point, Harry announced he wouldn't be in and would see them all on Monday.

Sue and Josh left at one. Both had things to do before they went to Penzance that evening to listen to their favourite folk group.

Kersty had a small pork pie and an apple, and worked on. At six-thirty she sat back, tired, stiff-shouldered, but satisfied. She had managed to finish everything she set out to do, and would take the contract with her this evening.

This evening. Each time she allowed herself even to think the words, her stomach churned with intoxicating excitement.

Stretching her arms to loosen her shoulders, she walked through to reception and looked out. The wet road was deserted. This was the lull between the last of shop workers going home and the emergence of the Saturday night entertainment seekers.

Locking the outer door, Kersty switched off the lights. Then, grabbing her bags, she hurried into the tiny kitchen and pulled down the blind.

Twenty minutes later she fastened the necklace around her throat and leaned forward to check the final effect in the small mirror propped above the sink.

Flushed with excitement, she had used the bare minimum of make-up, not trusting her unsteady hands. Mauve shadow on her lids enhanced her emerald eyes, and a touch of mascara had made her lashes seem twice as long. Beneath the rose lip-gloss, her mouth looked soft and inviting.

She had left her hair loose and it fell in a casual tumble to her shoulders, its mahogany sheen a perfect foil for the creamy skin of her throat and the vibrant colour of her dress which clung to her upper body, flaring from her hips into deep folds that swirled about her knees as she walked.

It was almost like looking at a stranger. With trembling fingers she touched the heavy golden links of her necklace. Then, drawing in a deep breath, she gathered up her scattered belongings and, sliding her arms into the padded jacket, turned out the light.

The rain had stopped. Broken clouds drifted like smoke across the flame-bright face of the setting sun as Kersty drove out of the town towards Ravenswood.

An echo from the past prompted her to stop and buy a bottle of good wine. Her mother had never allowed her to accept an invitation to anyone's house without ensuring she took along a small gift. Tonight was extra-special, and it seemed important to remember the small courtesy.

She drew the little car to a halt outside the cottage. Picking up her shoulder bag and the wine, she hesitated a moment, then grabbed the carrier as well. She would have to change before she went home. Neil would be the first to appreciate that, and would surely not mind her taking over his bathroom for a few minutes.

As she got out, careful on the unaccustomed high heels, the cottage door opened and Neil stood on the threshold.

Dark grey cords molded his hips, making his long legs look even longer. The sleeves of a pearl-grey turtle-necked sweater were pushed half-way up his forearms. It was obvious from the way the fine wool clung to his powerful shoulders that he wore nothing beneath it.

He watched, arms folded, as she approached. Her cheeks burned at the open admiration on his face. He waited until she reached the porch before saying softly, 'You've no idea how much I've looked forward to this evening.'

Kersty smiled into his eyes. 'Believe me, it can't be half as much as I have. I've even worn legs in honour of the occasion.'

'So I'd noticed.' He mouthed a soundless whistle and Kersty's colour heightened still further.

'I think you'd better take this before I drop it.' She thrust the wine at him.

As he stood back to allow her in, she noticed that his feet were bare. They were long, narrow feet with straight toes, the nails cut short and square. The gesture spoke of a special intimacy that thrilled even as she recognised, grinning at her own relief, that she could follow his example, discard her high heels, and really relax.

He stared at the bottle. 'What's this for?'

Placing her bags on the chair nearest the door, Kersty took off her jacket and dropped it on top of them.

'Well, I have heard,' she lifted her hair off her neck and shook it loose, 'though I don't know how much to believe, these rumours never lose in the telling, but the word is,' she paused, 'that you drink it.'

His head came up, eyes narrowed, and he transfixed her with a look that stopped her breath and set her blood racing.

Before she could blink he had set the bottle down and, almost lifting her off her feet, grasped her upper arms and caught her to him. Even with her heels on he still towered over her. The minty fragrance of his breath was warm on her cheek. His eyes glittered and his mouth curled in a slow, lazy smile.

'So that's the way it's going to be.' The throaty rasp sent an exquisite shiver down her spine. Every nerve was wire-taut with anticipation.

His gaze roamed her face. The smile faded, and hunger took its place. His fingers tightened. 'Oh, God,' he muttered, 'how I've missed you.'

'Neil,' she implored, 'kiss me.'

With a wordless sound, his mouth claimed hers. The sun sank slowly towards the horizon, birds twittered outside the window, a saucepan lid rattled softly in the kitchen.

Kersty was oblivious. Her entire world centred on the man whose strong arms enfolded her, whose lips and tongue were a sweet torment evoking a swelling ache of need even as they soothed her craving for his touch.

Eventually, warning pierced the languorous sensuality fogging her brain. 'Something's burning,' she murmured against his lips, her eyelids too heavy to open.

'Mmmm,' he growled, biting gently on her lower lip. 'Me.'

'No.' She struggled, her movements weak and uncoordinated as she tried to resist the soul-stirring magic of his mouth. 'Neil, I can smell it. Something really is burning.'

Lifting his head, he was utterly still for an instant. *'Damn!'* Letting her go so quickly that she staggered, he dashed into the kitchen and she heard the clatter of pans.

Smiling even as she tried to calm her ragged breathing, Kersty kicked off her shoes and moved on legs that felt like jelly to the window. She hugged her arms across her body, her breasts sore from being crushed against the hard-muscled wall of his chest.

The trees were stark black shapes against a burnt orange sky. In a few moments it would be dusk.

Gradually, her heartbeat returned to normal, the strange ache subsided and she was once more in control. Yet she knew it would take only one touch, one kiss, and she would melt.

Part of her was stunned by this previously unknown and unsuspected side to her nature, shocked at her own abandonment to the surging desire Neil aroused in her.

Yet how could she pretend she felt nothing? To deny this wondrous new experience was to deny not only what she felt for Neil, but her own femininity. And never before had she been so gloriously aware of herself as a woman.

She heard the pad of his bare feet on the carpet as he came up behind her. 'Kersty?' His voice was full of gentle concern. 'Are you all right?'

Turning her head, she smiled at him, radiantly happy. 'Never better.'

His relief was obvious. 'Forgive me, sweetheart. I didn't intend...it was just...'

Whirling swiftly to face him, she placed her fingertips on his lips to silence him. 'No apologies, Neil, no regrets. It takes two, you know,' she dimpled, half teasing, half sincere. 'I may lack experience, but I'm a very enthusiastic learner.'

The play of expressions across his face made her burst out laughing.

Smoothing her hair back, he cupped her face between his hands. 'You're wonderful.' His piercing gaze searched her face, as if he could hardly believe his luck. 'I've never met anyone quite like you. You're...' He hesitated, his eyes narrowing as he searched for the right words.

'Unique?' she supplied.

His expression was serious as he slowly nodded. 'Yes, Only once in a lifetime does a man meet a woman he— Kersty, I——' He stopped, compressing his lips as if to physically hold back words whose time had not yet come. Dropping a kiss on to the tip of her nose, he released her and, with his arm at her waist, guided her towards the table.

The polished oak was set with silver, lead crystal, white linen and, in the centre, a small vase of freesias.

'Forgive me. My selfishness is making me a lousy host. I haven't even offered you a drink, or thanked you properly for your gift, which I do, most sincerely. Would you like a glass of sherry?'

Kersty shook her head. 'No, thank you. Wine with the meal will be quite enough, especially as I'm driving home.' She felt momentarily disappointed and wished he had finished whatever it was he had started to say. But she knew better than to press him. He would tell her when he was ready.

Her spirits rose again. After all, there was no hurry. They had all the time in the world.

CHAPTER EIGHT

KERSTY set down her wineglass, rested her chin on her palms and sighed in deep contentment. The meal had been delicious, beef Stroganoff, served on a bed of fluffy rice, followed by a lemon sorbet. The haunting rippling notes of Chopin nocturnes were a perfect complement to the leaping flames and lamplight.

Leaning back in his chair, one arm on the table as he toyed with the stem of his wineglass, Neil watched her. 'A penny for them.'

Kersty smiled at him. 'They're worth far more than that.'

'Tell me, anyway.'

She closed her eyes for a moment. 'I haven't felt so relaxed in weeks. I'm utterly at peace with myself and the world.'

He raised his glass in salute. 'You couldn't have paid me a finer compliment.' He set the glass down again. 'I'll fetch the cheese and biscuits.'

She shook her head. 'Not for me, thanks. I couldn't. There simply isn't enough room.'

Neil frowned. 'Considering the amount of nervous and creative energy you burn up, you really should eat more.'

'How do you know what I eat?' Kersty countered. 'This is the first meal we've had together. For all you know, I might begin every day with a huge fry-up.'

'No, you don't,' he said at once. 'Well, maybe on Sundays, once in a while, when you're not rushing about.'

140

Kersty decided attack was the best form of defence. 'I dare say I'd find it only too easy to eat more if I had a Mrs Laity preparing all *my* meals.'

'Hold on!' He waved her down. 'Mrs Laity had nothing to do with this meal, other than shopping for the ingredients. I'll have you know I prepared the whole thing myself.'

'Really?' Kersty tried to sound sceptical, but couldn't hide her delight.

He grimaced. 'It took *hours*.'

'It was worth every second. Honestly, Neil, it was delicious.'

It was his turn for scepticism. 'Do I detect a note of surprise?'

'Only that you managed to find the time and the inclination to learn how to cook,' she responded with wide-eyed innocence.

'It was a matter of survival. I don't particularly enjoy eating out. The custom of sharing food in the context of a developing relationship is a private matter. Hotels and restaurants are naturally more concerned with the food and their profit margin.'

'So you do all your entertaining at home?' Kersty rubbed her finger slowly around the rim of her wineglass. The idea provoked very mixed feelings.

'No,' he said, and she glanced up in surprise.

'Business entertaining is done in the main house. Only one other woman besides you has been invited to dine here.'

Who? Kersty wondered and guiltily squashed the thought. It was none of her business.

'And yes, on rare occasions, if I'm particularly busy, Mrs Laity will prepare something. But mostly I fend for myself, and there are a limited number of ways to serve baked beans. So, I taught myself to cook. More wine?'

They talked on, serious, bantering and serious again, about food and the customs associated with it, about bureaucracy in general and local officialdom in particular. So the conversation returned to Ravenswood.

As Kersty left the table to fetch the contracts from her bag, Neil went to make the coffee.

'Go on over by the fire,' he directed. 'If we have to work this evening, we may as well do it in comfort.'

Kersty hesitated. 'Would you rather leave it? I mean, it's not really *urgent...*'

'Yes, it is,' he contradicted quietly. 'For your security and peace of mind. I do understand, Kersty.'

So, without conscious thought, she made herself comfortable on the hearthrug, her back against the sofa, toes pointed towards the blaze.

Neil snapped off the kitchen light as he came in with the coffee-pot. She glanced round, smiling up at him. It was only when he stood quite still, gazing at her with an unfathomable expression, that she realised her informality might be mistaken for presumption.

Quickly, she drew her legs under her, preparing to get up.

'No.' Neil's hand shot out. 'Stay where you are.' His voice softened. 'You look so... right.'

She sighed happily and straightened her legs once more. 'This is far more comfortable than home.' Her cheeks burned suddenly as all the interpretations of her totally honest, but impulsive remark dawned on her. *It had to be the wine.* She darted an embarrassed glance at Neil, but his back was to her as he poured the coffee.

Their empty cups sat side by side on the hearth, the signed contracts beside them on the carpet. Neil lay sprawled full-length on the sofa, his hands linked behind his head, a smile lifting the corners of his mouth. 'Now this,' he murmured contentedly, 'is living.' The record finished, the final notes dying to poignant silence.

Kersty turned to face him, laughter lighting her eyes. But, before she could speak, he caught her face and covered her mouth with his own. His lips were warm and tasted of wine and coffee.

Releasing her, he swung himself on to his feet and padded across to the stereo unit. Kersty swivelled round to watch him, resting her elbow on the sofa seat and her head on her palm. She loved the way he moved, smooth and sinuous, like a great cat.

Selecting a record, he put it on the turntable, pushed the switch, and the intoxicating rhythm of Latin America filled the room. Neil turned and held out his hand. A moment later she was in his arms.

Her feet had wings. She was one with the music. He held her as lightly as a feather and they moved in perfect harmony, separating and coming together as they swayed, dipped and turned. Time and time again they sought each other's gaze.

The track ended, they stood, poised, unmoving, then another began, slower this time. He gathered her to him, holding her close. Her head nestled into the curve of his shoulder and her arms slid lightly around his neck. Their feet barely moved. Neil bent his head to rest his cheek against her forehead and, as naturally as breathing, Kersty pressed her lips to his throat.

She felt his body harden as desire quickened from a smouldering ember into a living flame. A soft sigh caught in her throat as her bones melted to liquid sweetness and the strange ache returned, a throbbing emptiness crying soundlessly to be filled.

Suddenly, shockingly, Neil was gripping her shoulders, holding her away from him. She hung weak in his grasp, her eyes wide and unfocused, her mouth quivering.

'Kersty.' Her name was a groan, hoarse and strained in his throat. *'No.'*

'Why not?' The whispered plea was out before she could stop it. Then, even as the crimson tide flooded her face, she knew she hadn't wanted to stop it. She needed to know.

She could feel him trembling with the effort of control, the cost visible in the sweat that beaded his forehead and upper lip. 'I promised you time, and space.' He swallowed, his throat working. 'To make love to you now, this moment, would be the easiest thing in the world.' His gaze scalded her, his eyes burning with a passion that told her his need equalled, perhaps even surpassed her own. 'It would also be the most selfish act of my life.' His fingers tightened, bruising her flesh. 'I won't have you on my conscience, Kersty. It would be more than I could bear. Do you understand what I'm saying?' He shook her and she felt the desperation in him. 'I want you, God knows how much I want you, but——' He broke off, naked anguish distorting his features.

'It's too soon?' she whispered.

Some of the tension drained out of him. 'Do you understand?' He sounded more normal. He rubbed her arms gently in silent apology for his brutal handling. 'It has to be right for us. It's too important to risk...'

'It's all right,' she cut in, attempting a smile. 'Quite a turn-around, isn't it, a man having to fight for his virtue! I didn't know I was that sort of...' She broke off, suddenly overwhelmed by the aftermath of the intense physical and emotional upheaval she had just experienced. She knew he wasn't really rejecting her, yet that was what it felt like.

'Oh, Kersty,' he murmured, one arm around her shoulders, the other hand stroking her hair. 'My sweet, precious girl.' He kissed the top of her head. 'Come on. Get your coat.'

So soon? Somehow she swallowed her disappointment and stood back from him. 'I suppose it is getting rather late.'

Frowning, Neil looked at his watch. 'It's only half-past nine. Do you have to go yet?'

Kersty looked up at him in bewilderment. 'But I thought...I mean...don't you want me to leave?'

'Certainly not. Unless you feel you must.'

She shook her head quickly. 'I can manage another hour, if that's all right with you.'

'It's fine with me.' His face creased into a grin of relief. 'I should have made myself clearer. I just thought some fresh air might do us both good and...there's something I'd like you to see.'

Kersty stooped and picked up her high heels, one in each hand. 'Small problem.' She pulled a face.

'Ah.'

'Look,' she began hesitantly, 'I had to bring my work clothes with me. They're in the carrier. I changed at the studio. It—well—it seemed the most sensible thing. Perhaps it would be even more sensible if I changed back into my jeans and trainers now, especially if we're going to be stumbling around outside in the dark. What is it out there that's so important, anyway?'

'Wait and see.' He would not elaborate. 'You go and change. Use my room. First on the right at the top of the stairs. The bathroom's next door.'

As she stripped off her slip and tights, rolling them up with her dress, Kersty glanced around the room. It was undoubtedly a man's room, the muted colours, natural wood, and masses of books, devoid of ornament or frills. Yet it could almost have been *any* man's room. There was little of Neil's personality in it, no photographs, no clutter of odds and ends accumulated over the years, and Kersty heard the echo of Sue's observation. 'That one, he's all locked up inside himself.' Only the faint fragrance of his aftershave hanging in the air signalled his ownership, and there was a poignancy, almost a loneliness in the atmosphere.

Clad once more in her jeans and sweatshirt, Kersty thrust her dress and shoes into the carrier and, with a last look around, hoarding her impressions to relive later when she was once more alone, she hurried downstairs.

Neil was waiting by the door. He had donned his old flying-jacket and green Hunter boots, and carried a large flashlight.

His hands lingered for an instant on her shoulders as he helped her with her jacket, then he opened the door.

They stood in the porch for a few moments, waiting for their eyes to adjust, and Kersty realised it was not quite as dark as she had thought.

'Come on,' Neil took her hand and led her through the gap in the hedge, across the drive and into the trees. Now it was much blacker.

As he switched on the torch, the leaves rustled as some tiny scavenger fled from the beam of light. The trees loomed all around them, tall and ghostly, disappearing upwards into thick shadow.

They seemed to be climbing, then turned to one side as the ground in front of them fell steeply away.

A sudden scream chilled Kersty's blood, shock and fright bringing her heart to her mouth. She clutched Neil's hand with a strength she had not known she possessed, only to loosen her grip, overcome with relief and sheepishness, as on a whisper of white wings an owl glided over their heads, frozen for an instant in the light.

The night wind sighed through the trees, brushing leaf against leaf as the boughs creaked. Their footsteps made soft, shuffling sounds. With Neil in the lead they followed the narrow path that wound down the steep hillside.

Time and the darkness had distorted her memory, and Kersty had no idea where they were.

Neil had to bend his head and shoulders as they passed beneath an archway of rhododendron bushes so thick and intertwined that they formed a tunnel.

Then he stopped and switched off the torch. Kersty stood silent, waiting.

'Close your eyes,' he commanded softly. 'You'll come to no harm, I promise. Are they closed?'

'Can't you tell?' Her heart was beating fast. His arm around her shoulders held her tightly to his side as he guided her forward.

He didn't answer, and she sensed in the firmness of his grip a rising tension.

Now she was no longer concentrating on the torch beam or worrying about sliding on the steep, muddy path, all her other senses were coming into play.

The ground beneath her feet had changed again, from the springiness of leaf mould to a gritty firmness. She smelled the peaty richness of wet earth and heard the soft, steady drip of water from broad leaves. *Water.* She listened intently, and heard it, the chuckle of shallow water running over stones. *Could it be?*

Neil's arm tightened, halting her. 'You can open them now.' He sounded slightly hoarse.

Wraiths of cloud scudded swiftly across the milk-white face of a three-quarter moon whose cold light cast a luminous path on the tranquil surface of the lake. The trailing leaves of the weeping willow glistened with rain. Tall reeds fringed the water, dark silhouettes in a scene of black and silver.

The image shimmered, fragmenting like a broken mirror. Kersty turned her head and laid her cheek against Neil's hand on her shoulder. Her tears spilled over, and as they trickled over his fingers, Neil tilted her chin. 'I love you,' he whispered, but as she opened her mouth he covered it with his hand. 'No, don't say anything.' His voice was rough. 'I shouldn't have—dammit, I didn't intend——' He drew in a sharp breath.

'This has always been my very favourite place,' Kersty said softly, filled with radiant happiness. Her time would come, and when he was ready to listen she would tell him just how much he meant to her, how the attraction that had flared that very first day had, despite her very real fight against it, bloomed and deepened into love.

A love which, despite the differences between them, had grown deeper and stronger with each passing day.

'I wanted so much to ask you, but I was so afraid, and I didn't dare come back, in case it had...in case it was...' She turned her head, peering through the darkness.

'What is it?'

'The summer house,' Kersty said breathlessly, 'is it...?'

'Ah, yes, the summer house.' He led her along the path that edged the lake. His tone gave nothing away, and Kersty was filled with a mixture of hope, excitement and apprehension. 'When did you last see it?'

'I can't remember, years ago. I was still a child. The thatch was beginning to rot and the walls were crumbling. *Oh!*' she gasped as he switched on the torch. 'Oh, Neil!'

'I couldn't save the thatch, it had gone too far.'

The conical roof, with tiny slates at the apex graduating to larger ones that overhung the walls, sat on the little semi-circular house like a hat. The stonework had all been re-pointed, and a newly painted slatted seat was fixed all the way round the inner wall.

'Oh, it's *beautiful*,' she cried in delight.

'I did it myself,' he said, almost shyly. 'When I first saw it, it was virtually a ruin, the lake was choked with weed, the paths overgrown, but even then there was something about the place...I don't know. Anyway, the workmen had more than enough to do up at the house, so this became my special project. And I'd already decided, if anyone was going to carve their initials on the seat in the time-honoured fashion, it was going to be me,' his voice softened, growing deeper, 'when the right time and the right woman came along.'

As Kersty raised her face to his, her eyes moon-bright and radiant, a raindrop splashed on to her forehead, followed by another, and a third. All around they could hear the pitter-pat of rain falling in big, fat drops on to the leaves and the dark earth. The moon disappeared behind a thick blanket of cloud and the darkness took on a brooding quality.

Kersty shivered. 'Shall we run for it?'

'In a moment,' came the quick answer. 'First...' He drew her into the summer-house. It still smelt faintly of fresh paint. As the rain drummed on the roof and hissed into the lake, he slid one hand beneath her coat to draw her close, while the other caressed her face and hair as he brushed her lips with his own again and again.

When Kersty could no longer stand the exquisite torture, she seized his head, her fingers tangling in his hair and, as his arms tightened like steel bands around her, her mouth opened beneath his and she pledged him her heart and soul.

When at last she stood back, their ragged breathing was loud in the confined space. The rain had stopped, though water still ran from the leaves to drip steadily on to the ground.

'I think it's time you went home,' Neil's voice was rough.

I am home, she longed to say, but held the words back. He was not ready for her commitment yet. And, even as she fretted at the frustration of having to contain all the love she so longed to express, she blessed his thoughtfulness, his consideration for *her*. In any case, it made no difference whether she told him tonight, next week, or in a month's time—nothing was going to change.

Neil closed the door of the Mini and leaned down as Kersty wound the window open.

'Thank you for a fantastic evening.' She smiled up at him.

'The pleasure was mine.'

'Even the hours spent slaving over a hot stove?' she teased.

He grinned. 'But of course. Will you come again?'

'As soon as I'm invited.'

'I'll be in touch. In any case, I'll see you on Monday when you come to begin the filming. Though it will probably be a rather swift hello and goodbye. I've rather a busy week.'

Kersty made a wry face. 'I'm not exactly sorry. I don't find it terribly easy to concentrate when you're around, and with twenty thousand pounds of your money at stake, I need *all* my wits about me.'

'Stop worrying,' he chided gently. 'I have complete faith in you, and I'm the only one who matters.'

I love you. It almost spilled out. It was definitely time to go. She switched on the ignition. 'Thanks again, Neil, I enjoyed every moment.' With eyes and voice she tried to convey all that was in her heart, and knew from his burning gaze that she had succeeded.

'It was mutual. Drive carefully.' He straightened up and stepped back.

Kersty's last glimpse of him was his silhouette in the cottage doorway, one hand in his pocket, the other raised in farewell.

All the way home she hummed the tunes they had danced to, smiling to herself even as her fingers pressed against her midriff to ease the nagging pain, remembering . . . remembering.

The house was in darkness. Kersty let herself in quietly and crept through to the kitchen. Snapping on the light, she dropped her bags on one of the chairs. The carrier slid off and fell to the floor, spilling out her dress and shoes. Kersty sighed, hesitated, and with a dismissive wave, left it where it was and went to the cupboard for a glass and the bicarbonate of soda.

Shuddering at the taste, she was rinsing the glass when a sound behind her made her whirl round. Her father stood in the doorway, his blue woolen dressing gown tied haphazardly over his pyjamas, his hair tousled.

'Sorry, Dad.' Kersty set the glass upside-down on the draining-board. 'I didn't mean to wake you.'

'You're late tonight,' Stanley Hurrell observed. Catching sight of the things on the floor, he bent to pick them up.

'It's all right, Dad, I'll see to those,' Kersty said quickly, but her father had already lifted the dress, underwear and shoes back into the carrier and laid the bag on the kitchen table. They both looked at it.

'I see you've been out.'

'Yes.'

Kersty met her father's gaze and they stared at each other for a long moment. She could feel the tension tightening her muscles and the burn of acid in her stomach making the pain worse.

'With him?'

Her chin tilted. 'Yes.'

'I know, it's none of my business.' Her father's tone was sad rather than disapproving.

Kersty said nothing, but conflict raged inside her head. She felt guilty and hated it, not even sure *why* she was feeling that way. She was also resentful. Surely she was beyond the stage of having to answer to her father when she came in later than eleven o'clock?

'But, love, if he's genuinely fond of you, why the secrecy?'

'I don't know what——' she began, but the expression on her father's face dried the words in her throat.

'I may be getting old, but I'm not stupid, and I'll thank you to remember that, young lady,' Stanley Hurrell said with some asperity. 'Why didn't you come home to change? Why take your clothes to the studio, even though you have to come back through the village to get to Ravenswood? If you're so sure what you're doing is right, why hide it? Sneaking about as though you've something to be ashamed of.'

'It's not like that, Dad,' Kersty cried.

'Well, that's what it looks like from here.'

'You don't understand——'

'No, I don't,' he agreed. 'I know things have changed since I was young, but you're a grown woman, with a career and responsibilities.'

Kersty was bewildered, 'So?'

'So, where's your pride?' Her father demanded. 'Why can't he call for you here, like any normal, decent man would? Is he ashamed of you, or something?'

'Oh, Dad.' Half laughing, half crying, Kersty rushed forward and put her arms around her father. 'It isn't like that, really. The secrecy is for *my* sake, to avoid the Press. Neil has been through all that before, he knows how destructive it can be. He was only trying to make things easier for me. Dad, he's the kindest, funniest, most thoughtful man I've ever known. He *cares* about things...' She paused, then added, softly, 'About me.'

Her father held her at arm's length and studied her, frowning, concerned. 'You're in love with him.' It was a statement rather than a question.

She hesitated, remembering Neil's command that she tell no one of their relationship. But surely this was different? Her father certainly wouldn't tell anyone; he wasn't exactly over the moon about it himself, which, in its own peculiar way, was rather amusing.

She nodded.

'But you hardly know the man.' Again Stanley Hurrell seemed more worried than angry.

'Dad, you shouldn't make such sweeping statements,' Kersty reproached him gently. 'You have no idea how well I do, or don't, know Neil Drummond.'

Her father's gaze sharpened and Kersty felt her colour rise. Pride tilted her chin. 'And, no, I haven't been to bed with him. But only because *he* refused. He insists I need more time to be sure of my feelings. Is that the behaviour of a philandering playboy?' She controlled herself with an effort. 'Trust me, Dad,' she said quietly. 'I know what I'm doing.'

'I hope so, love. I dearly hope so.' But Stanley Hurrell's eyes, as they followed his daughter's departing figure, were clouded with concern.

Kersty held her breath as she drew back her bedroom curtains on Monday morning, and let it out in a rush of exultant relief at the clear pale blue sky. It was a fair bet that clouds would appear later, but if the forecast held true they would be the cotton wool balls that heralded a settled spell of dry weather.

After an early breakfast, Josh dashed off in his van to collect the lights from the hire company, while Kersty drove to the studio, dealt with the post, saw Dena settled in, and phoned the charter company to confirm the helicopter's time of arrival at Ravenswood.

She had just parked the Mini and was clambering out, clutching the storyboard, her shoulder-bag, jacket and keys, when Neil came round the side of the house. He was dressed in a formal, three-piece suit of pale grey, over a white shirt and mauve and grey striped tie. He looked preoccupied and, though the instant he caught sight of her his face broke into a smile, it was restrained and did not entirely banish his air of abstraction.

'Hi,' she greeted him, her own smile sympathetic. 'Problems?'

He looked startled for a moment, then shrugged lightly. 'I hope not, Kersty. I wish I could have been around more this week, but the way things are——' He gestured helplessly.

She grinned at him. 'I thought we'd been through all that and decided it was better if you weren't.'

He nodded slowly. 'Kersty, remember our bargain, and trust me. You do, don't you?'

The first thread of unease tugged. 'Of course. Neil, is something wrong?'

'Nothing I can't handle.' He fiddled with his cuff-links. 'I hope it all goes well today.'

Kersty glanced skyward. 'We've certainly got the weather for it. Just keep your fingers crossed there are no hitches.'

He smiled naturally for the first time. 'If there are, doubtless you will deal with them in your own inimitable way.'

'Is that a compliment?'

'You'd better believe it.' He glanced at his watch. 'I must go. Kersty?'

'Yes?'

He seemed about to speak, then a strange, shuttered look hardened his features. 'Good luck with the filming.' He turned and strode away.

Kersty stared after him, her smile fading to puzzlement as the conviction grew that his parting words were a substitute for what he had originally intended to say.

As Josh's van skidded to a halt on the gravel, a whirr of rotor blades above the engine noise announced the arrival of the helicopter.

Forcing Neil's unusual behaviour to the back of her mind, Kersty waved a greeting to her brother, then hurried round the side of the house to the lawn.

The Bell Jet Ranger in its livery of blue and white sat like a large insect on the smooth grass, the rotors circling slowly as the engine idled.

Jumping out, the pilot ducked to avoid the turbulence and came forward at a crouching run to meet her. He was a stocky, grizzled man in his mid-fifties, with deep creases etched at the sides of his eyes. 'Miss Hurrell? I'm Bob Crossley. Do you mind if we get started right away? Only, our other machine has developed gremlins in the fuel line, so I have an extra trip to fit in today.'

'We're ready when you are,' Kersty assured him as Josh panted up with the camera.

The Jet Ranger had been fitted with a special filming-door which had no glass.

'I hope you're wearing your thermals,' Kersty murmured, grinning, as her brother passed her to climb, under Bob's direction, into the back seat. As soon as the camera was safely fixed on to the special mount which would hold it secure and stable, Josh put his earphones on, adjusted his microphone and fastened his seat-belt. He gave Kersty a thumbs-up and, zipping her jacket, she climbed into the front seat beside Bob.

A few moments later they were airborne. The helicopter climbed vertically then, dipping its nose, surged forward and right in a sweeping curve. For one very uncomfortable moment Kersty felt as if she had left her stomach behind, and she swallowed hard.

But seconds later she had forgotten the brief unpleasantness in the thrill of actually flying. It was an incredible experience watching trees and fields rush by beneath her feet.

With an effort, she forced her mind back to business and switched on her microphone. 'OK, Josh?'

'Right on,' came the laconic reply. 'I'd like to do a complete circuit of the estate and get some long shots before deciding which angle of approach will give us the best over-view of the house.'

Kersty turned to the pilot. 'Is that all right with you?'

He nodded. 'Whatever you say, as long as we're back by eleven.'

'You hear that, Josh?' Kersty said, transfixed by the amazing view.

'Loud and clear. Now hush, and let me concentrate.'

Suppressing a smile, Kersty did as she was told. It was marvellous to be able to relax for a while and just enjoy being. The air was crystal-clear, washed clean by the previous day's rain. She could see the sea on three sides of the country, the waste tips of the china clay workings outside St Austell, and the vast shallow lake near the workings of Wheal Jane mine.

Over to her right was the town, its hotels and beaches fronting the open sea. The shops of the town centre were set back behind warehouses and wharves and piers fronting the river, and rows of houses sprawled over the hills between the two.

They veered north once more, over the village with its pub, chapel, school, four shops, smithy and huddle of houses, surrounded on three sides by farmland and on the fourth by the woods of the Ravenswood estate.

Kersty glimpsed a sleek white sports car speeding along the top road. The hood was down, revealing cherry-red upholstery. The woman driving had long, blonde hair, held back from her face by a scarf tied bandeau-fashion, the ends knotted below one ear, fluttering in the wind. She wore dark glasses and what looked like a flying-suit the colour of bitter chocolate.

'That's a Porsche Carrera.' Josh's voice was full of awe. 'Do you know they cost over *thirty thousand* new?'

'Josh, the film?' Kersty wailed.

'OK, OK, just broadening your education, that's all, showing you the sort of motor I'll be driving when I'm rich and famous.'

The car disappeared beneath a canopy of trees.

'If you don't get the shots I want, you won't live long enough to be rich and famous,' Kersty warned.

Bob swung the helicopter round in a huge circle. Then, with Josh giving instructions as to height and angle, began an approach that would carry them low over the house then rise to sweep round in a wide semicircle before coming in to land once more on the lawn.

'You happy with that, Kersty?' Josh added as an afterthought.

'It sounds great, and should make a tremendously effective opening sequence.'

'OK, folks, here we go.' Bob hauled the machine round and sent it swooping down. Kersty caught her breath. It was like being on a gigantic roller-coaster.

'Slow her down, Bob...a bit more,' Josh directed. 'Super job.'

They were following the drive through the park. Amid the fresh young green of the oak, ash and chestnut trees, the copper beeches glowed a rich purplish brown, and the bluebells, though past their best, were still an arresting sight as they rippled in the breeze.

Kersty caught the glint of sun on water. *The lake.* Memory stabbed, piercingly sweet, and she saw once again the moon-silvered surface of the lake, and heard Neil's voice, low-pitched and husky, telling her so unexpectedly that he loved her. Such precious moments were an oasis of tranquillity in their stress-filled lives, to be guarded and treasured.

Now they were approaching the house. Over the walled garden and vinery, to the right the newly converted craft units, and behind them, nestling in the trees, Neil's cottage. Then they were flying over the main roof. Below was a semicircular gravelled driveway where now three vehicles stood instead of two.

'Hey!' Josh's surprise and curiosity echoed vividly through the headphones. 'Isn't that the Porsche we saw earlier?'

Kersty didn't answer. She sat like a statue, staring straight ahead. No longer flesh and blood, but glass, and one word, one movement, would shatter her into a million pieces.

Her eyes were open, but they did not see the glorious panorama of garden or the elegant windows and sun-warmed granite wall of the house as Bob brought the Jet Ranger down to land as light as a feather on the grass. She still saw the couple standing on the gravel outside the massive front door. Neil, and a tall blonde wearing a chocolate-coloured flying-suit, dark glasses hanging carelessly from crimson-tipped fingers linked around his neck, as they stood, locked together in a passionate embrace.

CHAPTER NINE

'*KERSTY?*'

The sound of her brother's voice, laughing, impatient, pierced her daze and she looked up.

'At last! I thought you'd gone deaf.' His grin faded. 'Hey, are you OK? That last dive was a bit of a gut-churner. No offence,' he called over Kersty's head. The pilot raised a laconic hand.

'I'm all right. I'm fine.' Her voice sounded strange in her own ears. She climbed out of the helicopter. Her legs refused to support her and she clutched at the door, maintaining her balance with sheer effort of will.

'Thanks, Bob,' she said over her shoulder, forcing a smile. 'It was a fantastic flight.'

He nodded. 'Good day for it. Got your land-legs back yet?'

So he'd noticed. At least he didn't know the real reason for the treacherous weakness in her limbs.

Kersty reached for her clipboard as Josh finished unfastening the camera from the mount and shut the door. 'Yes, thanks.'

'OK, I'd better get moving. Hope to see you again some time.'

Josh caught Kersty's arm and pulled her out of the way as the rotor blades began to spin faster, whipping through the air with a swishing whine as the engine note rose.

The turbulence narrowed her eyes and plastered her jacket and sweatshirt to her body, streaming her hair out behind her. With a final wave, Bob lifted the Jet Ranger

159

off and, within moments, it had disappeared behind the trees.

Josh was keen, brisk. 'Right, what's next? I know we planned to do the inside work today, but it does seem a shame to waste this weather. How about finishing the exteriors today and move inside tomorrow?'

'Fine,' Kersty agreed vaguely.

Josh looked concerned. 'Are you *sure* you're all right? Shall I see if I can get you a drink or something?'

Kersty made a valiant effort to pull herself together. Her stomach felt as if it was on fire. 'Sorry, Josh, my mind was...' She gestured briefly. 'Let's get to work.'

She had to keep busy. More than anything, she wanted to run into the house and ask Neil what was going on. But that was out of the question. Apart from the fact that Neil had asked her to respect their bargain of secrecy, she couldn't sacrifice her pride and dignity in front of the blonde, whoever she was. She had to wait. And the only way she would survive the waiting was to keep so busy she wouldn't have time to think, to doubt, to worry.

Since the moment they had met, Neil Drummond had filled her every waking thought, but she hadn't realised just how frighteningly dependent her growing love for him had made her, until that shocking glimpse of the blonde woman twining herself around him and kissing him with such an air of possession. Suddenly the very foundations of her world were crumbling.

No! she screamed silently, wondering how she could hurt so much and yet continue to function normally. *It wasn't what it seemed. There was a simple explanation. Neil would explain. There was no threat.*

She followed Josh across the gravelled forecourt towards the van to collect the stills camera. But, before they reached it, Neil's blue Jaguar, a uniformed chauffeur at the wheel, purred in from the drive to stop outside the main door. It opened, and the blonde emerged, with Neil right behind her. The chauffeur got out of the Jaguar and crossed to the Porsche.

Was the blonde leaving? Kersty's heart thumped painfully against her ribs and her eyes flew to Neil. His expression was closed and unreadable.

'Could you both spare a moment?' he called, and the four of them came together in the centre of the forecourt. 'Charlotte, I want you to meet Kersty Hurrell, and this is her brother, Josh. He does the camerawork. Kersty, may I introduce Charlotte Ledbury, who will be running the marketing side of the project.'

Kersty's heart plummeted. Far from leaving, Charlotte Ledbury obviously planned to be around for some time, judging by the size of the two expensive suitcases the chauffeur had removed from the Porsche and was now carrying into the house.

From her highlighted hair and immaculate make-up, the jade silk shirt peeping from beneath the fine-grained leather flying-suit, to her matching high-heeled boots, Charlotte Ledbury radiated style, sophistication and wealth.

Kersty judged her to be between twenty-eight and thirty, and the golden cleavage just visible above the strategically lowered zip and unbuttoned shirt made her own slender figure seem sexless. Even the subtle perfume smelled so exclusive, Kersty knew she probably wouldn't even recognise the name. Her confidence shrivelled. She felt untidy and gauche.

The sky-blue gaze swept over her, calculating, assessing, and ultimately dismissive.

Her pride stung, Kersty's chin lifted. She held out her hand. 'How very nice to meet you . . .' She hesitated. To address the newcomer by her surname would undoubtedly maintain a formality and distance between them, and that appealed greatly to Kersty. But at the same time it would look as though she thought of herself as a subordinate. She didn't, and had no intention of allowing Charlotte Ledbury to assume that she did. Besides, it was only too obvious to anyone looking at the pair of them that the disadvantages were all on her side. 'Charlotte,' she finished.

There was a flicker in the other woman's eyes. She barely brushed Kersty's fingers with a long, elegant hand. Her smile, displaying small, perfect teeth, was cold and insincere. 'Neil was just talking about your work.' She flashed him an arch look. 'Darling, you didn't tell me she was quite so *young*.' The way she said the word invested it with several shades of meaning: *unsophisticated, inexperienced, untried*.

Kersty bit the inside of her cheek as her gaze flew swiftly, desperately, to Neil. The possessive endearment and Charlotte's familiar manner seemed to confirm the closeness of the relationship intimated by the kiss, a relationship that banished her, relegating her feelings to the level of an adolescent with a crush.

Neil's face was devoid of expression, his eyes opaque as they met Kersty's briefly, then moved deliberately on. *Trust me,* he had said. She would. She did.

'Age is irrelevant, Charlotte,' Neil said. 'Kersty is an extremely talented designer.'

Charlotte patted his arm in a proprietorial gesture and shook her head. 'You haven't changed a bit. Still generous to a fault. Darling, talent is all very well, but without a track-record, a proven credit list, and let's face it, this is hardly the hub of the universe, you're taking one hell of a gamble.'

'Possibly,' Neil agreed, blandly, 'but it's my money.'

Charlotte gave a disarming shrug as she turned to Kersty. 'No offence intended.'

Like hell, Kersty thought, but she smiled politely. 'None taken.'

'But I'm sure you see my point. I mean, we're talking business here.'

'Indeed,' Kersty nodded. 'Perhaps you weren't aware that my company has in fact, been operating for several years, during which time we've had some quite spectacular successes. Our client list, for a small concern, is quite impressive.'

'Really?' The single word was a masterly blend of surprise and scepticism. 'Now, isn't that odd? When I was making some enquiries a couple of days ago, having never heard of your company, I was told it was on the verge of folding, and almost certainly would have but for Neil's generous and timely intervention.'

Kersty swallowed hard. *Miles.* 'It never pays to listen to gossip, especially when it's based on malice and envy.'

'I'll be sure to keep that in mind,' Charlotte said in a tone that made it patently obvious she had no such intention. 'But I think it's time we got down to business. Neil, darling, I know you have simply masses of terribly important things to do, so why don't you leave Kersty, Josh and me to go over the details, and I'll bring you up to date at dinner tonight?' She flashed him a dazzling smile.

Neil's gaze met Kersty's.

Help me, she pleaded silently.

For an instant something stirred in the smoky depths of his eyes, then the curtain fell once more, shutting her out. 'Will you excuse me?' He glanced at his watch. 'I was due at a meeting ten minutes ago.'

'They're not likely to start without you,' Charlotte said playfully. 'After all, darling, you are Viscount Haldane.'

'That's hardly an excuse for being late, and even less of one for bad manners,' was his cool reply. With a brief nod that encompassed them all, he strode across to the Jaguar. As he shut the door, the powerful car was already pulling away.

Josh had been moving from one foot to the other in barely contained impatience for several moments, and Kersty sensed he was anxious to get back to work.

Charlotte turned a dazzling smile on him. 'Are you interested in cars, Josh?'

He blinked, then nodded, grinning. 'I wouldn't mind one like yours.'

'Not bad, is it? Do you fancy a spin?'

Josh goggled at her. 'You mean it?'

She nodded.

'Would I ever!'

'The keys are in the ignition. Help yourself. Not too long, though, I don't want to upset Kersty by keeping you from your work.'

That was precisely what she did want, Kersty realised. But why? Then it dawned. Charlotte had already tried sowing seeds of doubt about her in Neil's mind, now she was trying to drive a wedge between brother and sister. Charlotte wanted her to feel isolated, and the only possible reason had to be that she presented some sort of threat to Charlotte's plans for Neil.

There had obviously been a relationship between them in the past. Kersty's mind shied away from the precise details. She didn't want to know, it was more than she could bear. What was clear was that Charlotte clearly believed that the threads were ready to be picked up again. But why would she think that? *Unless Neil had encouraged it.*

No! Kersty could not accept that Neil would do such a thing. Not *now*. Not after they had become so close. Not after telling her he loved her. *Trust me,* he had said. So she would. If he knew the reason for Charlotte's behaviour, he would tell her when he could. If he didn't know, then it was up to her to try and ignore it, to believe in Neil and all that they had come to mean to one another. The very fact that Charlotte saw her as a threat was some small comfort.

All this flashed through Kersty's mind in seconds, some of it reasoned, most of it intuitive. She looked at her brother, who was hovering, clearly anxious to go, yet hesitant, knowing he should be working.

Kersty reached for the video camera. 'Well, what are you waiting for? You don't get an offer like this very often. Just don't forget what it cost you the last time you ran out of road.' She hid a grin as a fleeting shadow of disquiet marred Charlotte's indulgent smile.

'Spoilsport,' Josh called over his shoulder as he sprinted towards the sleek, expensive car.

Exultant at her small victory, her confidence gradually returning, Kersty turned to Charlotte, keeping her voice pleasant. 'I believe you wanted to go over the project details?' This war was not one of her making. But, while she would defend herself with whatever weapons that came to hand, she was not looking for a fight.

Charlotte's glance was quick and hard. An instant later she was all smiles. 'Let's go into the drawing-room. I'll have George bring us some coffee.'

With a pang, Kersty recalled her first sight of the elegant room, her nervous request for a glass of water, and George's unknowing revelation of Neil's true identity. It all seemed so long ago. So much had happened since.

George was crossing the hall as they walked in. As Charlotte opened her mouth to issue the order for coffee, he looked straight past her to Kersty. 'Miss Hurrell, how nice to see you again.' The genuine warmth in his voice touched and thrilled Kersty. 'His Lordship has spoken most highly of your work.'

'Th-thank you, George.' She glowed.

'And you'll no doubt be pleased to learn that a certain item has been repaired and is now functioning perfectly.'

Vividly recalling the embarrassing episode with the bell-pull, Kersty's cheeks bloomed with colour even as the corners of her mouth tilted upwards in an involuntary grin. 'Thank heavens for that.'

'Perhaps you'd care for coffee? His Lordship said you might be cold after your flight. If you and Miss Ledbury would care to go through to the drawing-room, I will ensure a tray is brought to you at once.'

'Thank you, George, that's very kind.' Kersty was barely able to contain her delight at Neil's thoughtfulness, and her surprise at George's reaction to Charlotte. Without in any way compromising his impeccable courtesy, he was making it abundantly clear that he didn't like her.

As they entered the drawing-room, the expression on Charlotte's face sent a shiver of foreboding down Kersty's spine, and her fingers strayed to the spot just below her breastbone where the burning pain gnawed.

When the coffee arrived a few minutes later, brought in by a uniformed waitress, Charlotte glanced up from the papers she had taken from a slim briefcase, frowned, and dismissed the girl curtly, saying they would help themselves.

Quickly, Kersty looked down at the storyboard on her lap, compressing her lips to obliterate any trace of a smile. Without even appearing, George had had the last word.

A few minutes later Josh breezed in to return the keys and collect the camera. 'Ah, coffee!' His eyes lit up. 'Super motor,' he grinned at Charlotte.

Her mouth twitched in a reflexive smile and she nodded briefly. 'Kersty, pour the coffee, would you? We really should get on.' She looked up from the pad on which she was making notes with a gold ballpoint.

Score one for Charlotte, Kersty thought to herself, relegating me to the status of maid.

'I take it you've no experience in marketing?'

'If I had,' Kersty answered carefully, 'there would have been no need to drag you all the way down here from London.'

'Thank God Neil had the good sense to do just that,' Charlotte muttered, frowning.

'You know him well, then?' Josh asked over the rim of his cup.

'Oh, yes,' Charlotte smiled, a secret, satisfied smile. 'Intimately, you might say.'

Kersty struggled to keep her face set in its expression of polite interest, as Charlotte went on, 'We go back years, Neil and I. In fact, I'm close to the whole family. I was friends with his two sisters before they married and went to live abroad.'

Kersty cleared her throat. 'Then you must have known his fiancée, too.'

Charlotte quickly masked her surprise, darted Kersty a swift, calculating glance, and leaned forward to pick up her coffee. 'Yes, I knew Phillipa, though not well; she certainly wasn't part of our set. Of course, it wasn't a love match, more one of those family things. Poor Phillipa,' Charlotte sighed, 'such a little mouse. Dying like that was her one moment of glory.' Kersty flinched at the total insensitivity of Charlotte's offhand remark. 'It was very sad and all that,' Charlotte added, 'but not as sad as if she'd married him.'

'What makes you say that?' Josh was openly curious, looking at her over the rim of his cup.

'Because it wouldn't have lasted. She was so completely wrong for him. She was ridiculously shy for a start. She scarcely ever opened her mouth except to talk to *him*. I mean, it was a terrible burden for the poor man. She was such a bore. Her only interests were gardening and cooking and looking after other people's children.' Charlotte's mouth curled in disdain. 'She probably wanted a dozen of her own. Just a typical housewife.'

Yet she had been quite prepared to fly to the heat and humidity of the Brazilian rain forest to spend two weeks with Neil, Kersty remembered.

For the quiet, home-loving girl Charlotte's scathing words conjured up, such a journey must surely have taken a great deal of courage, and love.

'From what I know of him,' Kersty said carefully, 'Viscount Haldane doesn't appear the sort of man to propose marriage to someone who bored him.'

'But then, you *don't* know him, do you?' Charlotte's smile was pure vitriol. 'Take my word for it, Phillipa was Neil's concession to family pressure. Still, things are different now. Personally, I think Neil carried this mourning business too far. Three years is a long time. Far too long for a man of his...' She paused knowingly '...passionate nature.'

'Ah!' Josh grinned uncertainly, and Kersty saw unease beneath his effort to appear a man of the world. 'So this isn't just a business trip?'

Charlotte laid a long crimson-nailed finger against her full lips. 'I really mustn't say anything else. But look at it this way: I'm staying here at the house, and will be acting as Neil's hostess for all the social events that will be part of the launch.' She shrugged gracefully. 'People must draw their own conclusions.' She tossed a folded newspaper with studied casualness on to the sofa between Josh and Kersty. 'The Press seem to have got wind of it already. I can't imagine how.'

I bet you can't, Kersty thought savagely. But the momentary flare of violence was smothered beneath a suffocating blanket of helplessness. She felt like a small boat adrift on a stormy, shoal-ridden sea, powerless, at the mercy of wind, current and the jagged rocks waiting just below the surface to destroy her.

'Still,' Charlotte said, 'it's all marvellous publicity for the project.'

'Well, open it, Kersty,' Josh urged. He put his cup down. 'Here, let me.' He rifled the pages. 'Wow, that's some photograph.'

Charlotte shrugged. 'Patrick never takes a bad one.'

'Lichfield?' Josh gaped.

'Is there another?' Charlotte responded with a patronising smile.

Josh's eyes darted along the lines of print. 'The article certainly doesn't pull any punches,' he muttered, then glanced up, puzzled. 'But the project is hardly mentioned.' He passed the paper to Kersty, picked up the video camera and started adjusting the focus and distance, a clear sign he wanted to be out of a situation he did not understand and which made him uncomfortable.

Kersty skimmed through the article, a masterpiece of innuendo and arch questions concerning Charlotte's arrival at Viscount Haldane's estate. She refolded the paper and laid it aside.

'No comment, Kersty?' Charlotte's gaze was bright with malice.

Kersty felt chilled to her soul. Neil must have seen the paper. If he hadn't read it before Charlotte's arrival, she would certainly have shown it to him.

Realising her silence was betraying the turmoil within her, Kersty forced a smile. 'It's a stunning photograph,' she said truthfully. 'How fortunate the Press library had such a recent one. As for the article, it's not the way I would have approached the launch of the project, but,' she gestured with one hand, 'as we both know, I'm no marketing expert. If his Lordship approves of your methods, my opinion is really of no importance.'

Charlotte's smile was smug. 'Oh, Neil was quite happy with it.'

Kersty swallowed. It didn't add up. He had been almost paranoid about the need to keep his relationship with *her* a secret. To protect her, he had said, and she had been grateful. *But had that been the real reason?* His insistence on secrecy took on an entirely different significance now Charlotte Ledbury had arrived on the scene to stake her claim, both professional *and personal* to Neil Drummond.

Doubts were beginning to flood in. For each one she banished, another reared up to take its place.

The rest of the day was a living nightmare. Charlotte queried every one of Kersty's decisions concerning the video. Some of the criticisms were indeed justified, and Kersty could have accepted them quite easily had it not been for Charlotte's patronising impatience and deliberate attempt to belittle all her ideas and undermine her confidence.

Nor did it end when she got home; Stanley Hurrell thrust the newspaper under her nose. 'Have you seen this?' He flung it across the table in disgust. 'I warned you, didn't I?'

Kersty nodded. 'Yes, Dad. You warned me. You really want to believe it, don't you?'

'Kersty, love, I don't want to see you hurt. Oh, I don't blame the man. I suppose he has women flinging themselves at him all the time. I dare say he knows how to handle it. But what about you? If he cared as much as you seem to think he did, would he have allowed his name to be used like that?'

She was about to argue, to point out that Neil wasn't responsible for what other people implied, when it struck her that her father was using the past tense as if whatever there might have been between Neil and herself was now over, finished.

Trust me.

The next day was even worse. There was no sign of Neil when they arrived to start the interior filming nor did he appear later. The phone rang constantly, and the brief glimpses she caught of George revealed rare ill-humour visible in his tight-lipped expression. The atmosphere in the beautiful house was unpleasantly charged as staff hurried, grim-faced, about their duties.

Kersty felt sick with tension and misery. She threw herself into her work, checking and adapting the storyboard, helping Josh move and set up the lights, concentrating so fiercely on *not* allowing Charlotte to provoke her into rudeness or temper that by five she had a raging headache.

'What is there left to do?' Charlotte queried, covering a bored yawn with her talon-like fingertips. 'I'm really quite exhausted.'

'Only the vinery,' Kersty replied. 'I want a shot of the pool for the brochure.'

Charlotte brightened immediately. 'It will be far more effective if someone is actually using it, or better still, in the jacuzzi. I'll just go and get my bikini.' She disappeared in a whirl of silk suit and expensive perfume.

Josh glanced round to make sure no one else was around. 'I won't be sorry to get out of here,' he confided.

Kersty knew exactly what he meant. She longed to tell him how different it had been the first day she came. How welcoming the house had seemed. But what was the point? It wasn't any more. Nothing was the same any more. *Why hadn't Neil been in touch?*

She felt something tear inside her. Stupid question, and the answer was all too obvious.

Trust me. She was clinging on by her fingernails, but her grip was slipping.

Charlotte insisted Josh take several shots of her, beside the pool, in the pool and in the jacuzzi. She had piled her hair high on her head and arranged delicate, curling tendrils to enhance the graceful line of her throat.

'What *is* this?' Josh muttered resentfully as he passed Kersty, responding to Charlotte's demand for a close-up, the white, foaming water bubbling around the golden skin of her shoulders and breasts, her bikini top out of sight, suggesting she was naked in the water. 'Are we doing a hotel brochure or glamour shots?'

Kersty didn't reply.

'Right, I'm off,' Josh announced flatly as Charlotte, wrapped in a fluffy towelling robe, disappeared into the main house. 'I'll return the lights to the hire company

after I've had my tea; they're open till eight. You know,'
he paused, thoughtful, 'I was quite taken with Charlotte
that first day, but now, I don't know, there's something
about her...she certainly seems to know her job, but...'
He shrugged. 'I'm glad Sue's not like that.'

For the first time in two days, Kersty's smile was un-
forced. 'I was beginning to wonder if you'd ever realise
just how lucky you are.'

Josh grinned. ''Course I do, but I can't risk her getting
big-headed.'

'With a chauvinist piglet like you?' Kersty scoffed.
'Fat chance.'

Josh looked pensive. 'What's so great about a Porsche,
anyway?' He added softly, 'Personally, I think his
Lordship wants his head looked at.' He finished putting
the camera into its case. 'What are you doing tonight?'

Kersty's head throbbed dully. To go home would mean
either questions or sympathetic silence from her father.
She could not face that. 'I think I'll go back to the studio
and start on the script. It'll be quiet, and with no inter-
ruptions I should get quite a bit done. Tell Dad for me,
will you?'

'What about a meal?'

'I'll pick something up on the way,' she lied. She felt
queasy already. The thought of eating made her stomach
heave.

Kersty stared at the scene frozen on the monitor. This
was the fourth time she had replayed it. If she looked
at it long enough, it would lose its capacity to hurt. She
would become immune, numb, incapable of feeling. That
was the theory. Only it wasn't working.

So brief, only a few frames, it lasted two seconds at
most. Josh hadn't even noticed it happening, his attention riveted on the sports car. As for the pilot, if he'd
seen it, he had obviously considered it none of his
business.

you needn't be, honestly. The film is fantastic, the photographs are beautiful, and the brochure is the best you've ever done. You know all that without me telling you, so why are you driving yourself like this? His Lordship can't help but be delighted. Dena is certainly impressed, and she's worked on bigger projects than this. Kersty, you've got to ease off.'

'Honestly, Sue, you do fuss,' Kersty retorted with a lightness that rang horribly false even to her own ears. 'I can't possibly leave it now I'm so close to finishing. Once it's done, *then* I'll take a break.'

'Promise?' Sue's small face was serious.

'Mmm.' Kersty nodded, her gaze sliding away from the girl's patent concern, wishing she would go. Why wouldn't they all just leave her alone?

With a muttered sound of frustration she switched off the microphone and ran the master tape back for the fifth time. For God's sake, the sentence was only half a dozen words long. Why couldn't she get it right?

The pain in her stomach was distracting her, that was the problem. She'd soon sort that out.

Reaching for her bag, Kersty opened it and looked inside for the packet of mint-flavoured indigestion tablets. There it was, in the corner. As she reached in, her fingers encountered a cork.

For an instant she wondered, then memory drenched her like an ice-cold wave, leaving her breathless and shaking. The champagne celebration on her return from Ravenswood the day she had discovered Neil was Viscount Haldane.

She snatched her hand away and the bag fell sideways, spilling some of its contents: her small appointments book, her car keys, the box of mints, and a folded white handkerchief. Neil's handkerchief, with which he had protected the wound in her back the day they met.

Kersty thrust everything but the mints back into her bag and pushed it out of the way. She couldn't think

about it now. She *wouldn't* think. She had work to do.
That was all that mattered. Work. Quickly, she crunched
two of the tablets between her teeth, shuddering as she
swallowed the chalky, glutinous mess.

Clearing her throat, she reset the stopwatch, pressed
the switch to start the videotape again and, as the aerial
view of the house came up on the screen, almost the last
scene, she thumbed the watch button and started to
speak, but the sound that emerged was strained and
tremulous.

'*Damn!*' she croaked, throwing mike and stopwatch
on to the console. She buried her face in her hands.
'Damn, damn, *damn*!' Her shoulders began to shake
and a racking sob tore itself loose from her throat. She
couldn't hold it back any longer, couldn't pretend any
more that everything would be all right.

Worse than the physical pain was her heart's agony.
Yet even now she still could not, would not accept what
seemed the only explanation for Neil's total absence from
her life this past week, that to him she had been merely
a diversion, a brief excursion into different emotional
territory, an experiment.

Clinging to the memory of the precious hours they
had shared, hours during which he had awakened her
to the glorious reality of a man's love, made her see
herself through his eyes, a beautiful, desirable woman,
hours of joy sharing memories of the past and hopes
for the future, she had clung also to belief and trust.

Hadn't she told him—how long ago it seemed—that
if you really believed in something then you fought for
it?

She had fought. She had fought her own doubts and
fears. The feeling of being threatened by Charlotte had
been much harder to fight. But she had tried, forcing
herself to believe there was no personal enmity in the
constant criticism of her work, the impatience, the
scathing comment designed, like a stiletto blade, to leave

barely a mark on the surface, while wounding deep. With all her strength she had resisted the other woman's determined efforts to crush her spirit, reasoning that Charlotte's malice had to be born of fear. For such behaviour would surely be unnecessary if she was as well established in Neil's life as she claimed to be.

But in the face of constant, unremitting pressure both at the studio and at home from her father, the endless extra work Charlotte deemed necessary, plus her own feelings of inadequacy running riot in the absence of Neil's reassurance, her strength had finally run out.

Physically and emotionally exhausted, she wept, her salt tears adding their own cruel sting to her lacerated self-esteem. At least there was no one here to witness her final admission of defeat.

'Kersty?'

She froze, hunched over in pain and misery.

'Kersty?' *Neil's voice?* 'You know you shouldn't leave that outside door unlocked at night, anyone could walk in.'

Twisting round in her chair, her face hot and wet with tears, she gulped back a sob as he strode into the editing-room.

'What are you doing?' He sounded astonished.

The only light came from an anglepoise lamp above the console. Never had Kersty been so grateful for the deep shadows it cast. Turning her back on him, she fumbled in her bag for a tissue. Her heart hammered so loudly, it almost deafened her. *He was here. He had come at last,* and she loved him and hated him in the same instant. Unable to find the tissues, her nose beginning to run, she grabbed the folded handkerchief she had always meant to return but somehow never remembered. Swiftly, she wiped her nose and eyes. 'What does it look like?' she retorted, her voice thick with pain and grief.

'It looks as though you're working,' he grated, 'and I want to know why. I've rung here three times in the past hour and got no reply. I've a drawing-room full of people back at Ravenswood to whom I'm supposed to be playing host. Charlotte tells me you turned down your invitation because you had a date——' his icy tones sent a shaft of real fear through Kersty '—and when I tried to reach you at home, your father told me in no uncertain terms to stay away from you. Now, what the hell is going on?'

Kersty leapt to her feet, the movement so sudden that it sent her chair cannoning back against the wall. She whirled round on him, fists clenched. 'Don't you *dare* take that tone with me!' she hissed, almost incoherent under the stress of violently conflicting emotions that seemed to be tearing her apart. 'I don't know what you're talking about. I haven't heard a word from you for six days. Not a note or a phone call, and certainly no invitation to any party. And as for *me* having a date——' her eyes flashed green fire at the injustice of his accusation '—I've spent eighteen hours a day for the past five days right here in this studio doing all the extra work *your*—girlfriend insisted was necessary before she could accept the project. So you tell *me* what's—aaagh!' She doubled over, clutching her midriff as white-hot pain lanced through her.

'Kersty?' In two steps he was beside her. Snatching up the lamp, he directed it on to her ashen face, saw the dark smudges beneath her closed eyes, and the hair on her forehead and temples dark and damp with sweat.

A vicious expletive escaped his lips and, slamming down the lamp, he caught her upper arms. 'Kersty? What's wrong? Are you ill?'

'Don't worry,' she muttered through gritted teeth, 'the project won't suffer.' There was a roaring in her ears, and the walls seemed to be closing in then retreating.

'I'll see it finished if I have to crawl into the studio. I keep my word.' Her own voice sounded far away.

'Damn the project!' he shouted. 'Kersty?' he forced her chin up. 'For the love of God, tell me what's the matter—you look dreadful.'

'Thanks.' It was meant to be ironic, but the flaring anger that had given her brief strength drained away like water down a sink, leaving her weak and shaking. 'Neil?' She clutched at him as her legs gave way. 'I—I——' With a small sigh, she crumpled and would have fallen.

Vaguely, she felt herself swept up into strong arms and carried. She was placed on a chair, her head almost on her knees, and seconds later a cold, wet cloth bathed her face and the back of her neck.

As she returned to full consciousness, she sensed bitter rage emanating from the grim-faced man who crouched in front of her. She raised her head and looked into blue eyes as cold and hard as splinters of ice.

'Are you strong enough to stand?' he demanded tersely. She nodded. 'Right, stay where you are. I'll fetch your bag and coat. I'm taking you to the hospital.'

Kersty was aghast. 'Y-you can't. I-I'm all right now.'

'Have you had the pains long?' he queried flatly, one dark brow raised, his gaze fixed on Kersty's hand, as, unconsciously, she pressed her fingers to the gnawing ache.

Flushing, she snatched it away, clasping her hands tightly in her lap. 'It's indigestion, that's all.' She was adamant, her mind totally closed to reason or argument. 'Anyway, what about your party? All those important people?'

'To hell with them,' he snarled. 'There's no one more important than you.' He straightened up, raking his hair with an unsteady hand, talking almost to himself. 'I never intended it to go this far. God damn it, I should have *known*——' His features were bleak with self-disgust.

'What are you talking about?' Kersty felt unease slither along her veins, damping the spark ignited by his assertion of her importance.

'Never mind, I'll explain later.'

She shook her head. 'You'll explain now. I'm not going anywhere with you until you do.'

'Kersty, all this can wait...'

'No, it can't,' she cried. 'I haven't seen you for days. Every time I tried to phone I was told you were away or unavailable. Now you march in here and start ordering me around. It won't do, Neil. I'm not putting up with it. I don't know where I am any more.'

He said quietly. 'I assume you believe this has something to do with Charlotte?'

Kersty laughed. It was harsh, high-pitched and full of pain. 'You could say that. From the moment she arrived she made it perfectly clear to Josh and I that the pair of you were old...*friends*, and that she was here, at your request, to pick up the threads and weave them into a much closer,' Kersty's voice wobbled and she fought to hold it steady, 'more permanent relationship.'

Neil's voice was quiet, and for an instant Kersty thought she detected despair. 'And you believed her?'

'No, I didn't. Not at first. It didn't tie up with the way things were between us. But as the days went by...' Kersty's throat stiffened with tears as she relived the terrible loneliness, far worse than anything she had ever experienced over Martin's defection. 'She appeared to have your full approval for all the alterations and extra work, plus free run of the house. Then there was that article in the paper...and you were never there. She even...' Kersty shrugged and her face contorted for an instant. 'She even knew what was in the notes I left for you that you never answered.'

His face was thunderous. 'What notes?'

'When I couldn't reach you on the phone, I left two letters, one in your office in the house, the other at the cottage.'

His jaw tightened. 'So that's what Mrs Laity meant,' he muttered.

'What?'

His eyes glittered as they met Kersty's. 'Mrs Laity told me, rather nervously, that Charlotte had warned her there was a young woman, who apparently had a crush on me, making a nuisance of herself. If Mrs Laity came across any notes or letters addressed to me, she was to give them to Charlotte, who had my authority to destroy them.'

Kersty stared at him, horrified. 'And you knew about this?'

'No, of course I didn't,' he snapped. He was pacing the small kitchen like a caged animal. 'I *did* know she would be likely to boast about our past relationship, though it scarcely warrants the term. We met at a party. She'd just ended an affair and was looking for someone to move in with. Charlotte was a high-flyer and the title was an added incentive. She told me she was a friend of my sisters. I was lonely, bored and I'd had too much to drink. We spent the night together. She seemed to think that somehow sealed our future. It took me two very difficult and unpleasant weeks to put her straight.'

Kersty watched him as he paced. 'Yet you hired her to do the marketing.'

'No.' He shook his head. 'I know the chap who runs the agency. He's brilliant and the agency is very much in demand. They only employ top-rate people. I imagine Charlotte heard about the commission and suggested herself for it on the strength of knowing me personally.'

Kersty's forehead puckered in bewilderment. 'But if you wanted nothing more to do with her, why did you allow her to stay?'

Neil stopped his pacing and stood quite still, his back to her, one hand in the trouser pocket of his dark suit. With the other, he slowly rubbed the back of his neck. Then he swung round to face her. 'Because she suited my purpose on two counts. One, she obviously knew her job and was just the marketing expert we needed, and two,' he hesitated, 'I guessed that when she met you, she would lay it on thick about what she and I once meant to each other. She was also quick off the mark getting it into the paper.' He swallowed. 'I wanted to be sure you could handle it.'

Kersty stared up at him, her eyes huge, her face drained of colour. 'You *deliberately* put me through all this?' she croaked. '*Why*, for pity's sake? Wasn't it enough that I loved you?'

'You *thought* you loved me,' he grated. 'But we haven't known each other very long, and because I wanted to give you time to be sure, our relationship has been...limited. I had to be sure you would be able to cope with the inevitable gossip and muck-raking. Kersty, I'm thirty-six years old. I'm no playboy, but I've had my fair share of women. One or two I really cared for. The others——' He shrugged. 'We were both consenting adults and it was fun at the time.' A note of strain entered his voice. 'But you were different. From the moment we met I knew you were special. You were what I had been waiting for all my life. Someone who understood what I was trying to do here and how much it meant to me. Someone I could admire and respect. But the moment our relationship became known, the gutter press would have a field day raking over my past and paying girls like Charlotte large sums of money for kiss-and-tell revelations about the sexual preferences of Viscount Haldane.' His voice was bitter with disgust. 'If you couldn't cope with it, what was the point of putting either of us through that kind of ordeal?'

The silence was heavy. Kersty stared at him, her throat working. 'You bastard,' she whispered, and the pain tore and clawed at her like barbs, doubling her over with a gasp.

'Hospital, *now*,' he rapped. He grabbed her coat from the back of the door.

'I must phone Dad,' she gasped.

'Leave your father to me,' Neil said grimly. 'He has some explaining to do, such as why he never passed on my phone messages to you.'

Kersty's head jerked up, her face grey. *'What?'*

'Later,' he said abruptly. 'I promise I'll telephone him, Kersty. I'll do it while you're in with the doctor.'

With his arm around her, warm and supportive, he led her out into reception, switching off the lights and closing doors on the way.

'Just a minute.' Kersty hobbled across the desk.

'What is it?' Neil was impatient.

'I just wanted to check...' Kersty glanced round at him. 'The phone wasn't switched through to the studio. I had both doors closed. That's why I didn't hear it when you rang earlier.'

'Never mind that now.' Just as he reached for her the telephone trilled. They both jumped.

Automatically, Kersty put out her hand, but Neil was quicker. He lifted the receiver. 'Yes?' His tone was curt.

Kersty could hear Charlotte's cut-glass tones clearly, and detected apprehension.

'Darling, at last. What on earth are you doing *there*? You really should be here, you know. I'm doing my best to keep everyone happy, but George is sulking and the maids are never around when you want them——'

'Charlotte.' The single word cut her off in mid-sentence. Kersty had never seen him so angry. But it was a contained anger, cold, quiet, and deadly. 'If you value your job, you will be out of my house and off my property within the hour.' Kersty heard her gasp. Neil took not the slightest notice. 'I want your replacement, preferably male, here by Monday morning. If this isn't done, I shall take my business to another agency and make certain your boss knows why. If you mention my name or those of my staff, friends, or business associates to the Press in any context whatever, I shall sue you to hell and beyond. Now, put George on the line.'

Kersty heard the receiver clatter on to the table. Which category did she fit into, she wondered dully, staff or business associate? She couldn't be a friend. Friends were trusted. But Neil hadn't trusted her. He'd had to test her. She started to turn away, but Neil caught her arm and drew her to his side. She didn't have the strength to fight. *Besides, God help her, it felt so good to be close to him again.*

'George? Make sure everyone has a drink and something to eat and give them my apologies. I've been called away on an emergency.' He listened for a moment, holding the phone very close to his ear so Kersty could not hear what George was saying. 'No, not tonight. And cancel all tomorrow's appointments, will you? One more thing, George, Miss Ledbury has been given one hour to get off the estate.' He listened again then said drily, 'Yes, I'm sure you will. Thank you. Goodnight.' He replaced the receiver and looked down at Kersty. 'Come on,' he said softly, 'let's go and get you sorted out. And on the way I'll tell you how I got on in London.'

Her eyes widened. 'London?'

'I've been away for four days. A series of business meetings, plus the final settlement of my father's estate. I now have all the money I need to fulfil my plans for Ravenswood. I only got back this morning.'

'Oh,' she gulped. No wonder she hadn't seen him. No wonder Charlotte had been making so free with the house and staff. *Neil had not been there.*

As he turned the key and the Jaguar purred into life, Kersty said in a small, tight voice, 'I don't want to go.

Please, Neil, just take me home. I'm all right now. I feel heaps better. I'd rather go home.'

She felt his gaze on her. She couldn't look up, couldn't meet his eyes, couldn't tell him her *real* fear. But somehow he knew.

'It will be all right,' he promised. 'I'll stay with you.'

'They might not let you,' she whispered.

'Oh, they will,' he said drily, and turned the car on to the road.

And so they had. When Kersty emerged from the changing cubicle after the most thorough medical examination she had ever undergone, Neil was waiting for her, smiling. She searched his eyes, but there was no shadow, no reservation. 'I'm—it's all right?' It was funny how she looked at him rather than the doctor. But Neil wouldn't lie. *She could trust him.* The realisation broke over her like the sun through cloud. It warmed her very bones and thawed her frozen heart.

'There's nothing, Kersty,' he reassured her. 'Stress and lack of proper food have caused severe inflammation. But there's no ulcer, though you were heading for one, and *nothing else at all.*'

She bent her head to hide the quick rush of tears.

'You've a lot to be thankful for, young lady,' the doctor said, 'you're strong and healthy. But you can't go on the way you have been...'

Kersty wasn't listening. Clasped in Neil's arms, her face buried in his neck, she clung to him. 'I was so afraid,' she whispered into his collar. 'My mother...'

'It's all right,' he soothed. 'I'll take you home.'

Kersty huddled into the corner of the sofa, staring at the leaping flames. The scent of applewood filled the room. She looked up as Neil came in from the kitchen carrying a tray with two mugs on it and a plate of flapjacks.

'I thought you meant my home.'

'There's no one to look after you there.' He set the tray on a table alongside the sofa.

'I don't need looking after,' she retorted automatically. 'I'm perfectly capable——'

'Yes, of course you are.' Neil's tone was heavy with irony. 'You're overworked, overtired, underfed and have just been through an emotional wringer,' his voice softened, 'not to mention the dreadful burden of fear you've been carrying. Yes, you're doing just fine.'

Tears of exhaustion welled in Kersty's eyes. 'And you're a bully,' she retorted, her voice ragged.

'I haven't even started. Drink this.' He passed her one of the mugs. Filled to the brim, it had a creamy foam on top.

'What is it?' she demanded suspiciously.

'Egg, milk, honey and a large dollop of brandy. It's the best restorative I know. My mother swears by it. She's coming down for a short holiday in a couple of weeks. She'll certainly notice some changes since her last visit.' He glanced at Kersty. 'She stayed here with me at the cottage last time.'

Kersty stiffened momentarily as she realised the significance of what he was saying. *Only one other woman besides you has ever been invited here.*

'Anyway,' he said, 'you should be feeling better by then, and you'll have had time to reach some decisions.'

'About what?' She sipped the creamy liquid. It slid down her throat like nectar, warming and soothing her tender stomach, unravelling the tension which for so long had wound her nerves tight.

Neil rested his elbows on his knees, cradling the mug as he stared at its contents. He seemed suddenly on edge. 'You know how much I admire your talent as an artist. You've built up a small but highly thought-of business, and now you've taken on another designer and sorted out the financial problems, you'll be able to broaden your scope and expand. I mean, if that's what you *want* to do.'

Kersty stared at him, confused. 'What are you talking about?'

He shot her a sidelong glance. 'An alternative. You—you could——' he made a small gesture with the mug '—throw in with me. Your organisational and artistic abilities would be invaluable. You know the village people and they know you. Obviously that would make things so much easier all round. Look,' his voice was taut and strained, 'you don't have to decide right now. You've been through a lot lately, and I'm responsible for much of it. I—I know I don't deserve it, Kersty, but I want the chance to put things right.'

With a business partnership? She caught her lower lip between her teeth, biting savagely to stop the tell-tale quivering. She shook her head. 'I—can't,' she whispered.

'Why not?' he pleaded hoarsely. You love...Ravenswood. Please—think of what you're turning down.'

She knew only too well. But how could she accept? She had dreamed, romantic, foolish dreams. His offer was genuine, of that she was certain. It was also impossible to agree to.

'We——' She swallowed hard, but the lump in her throat refused to budge. 'We want different things,' she managed at last.

'That's not the impression I got.' He stood up, slamming his mug down on the mantelpiece with such force that his coffee slopped over and ran down the outside, to form a pool. 'In fact, I don't believe it. I know how you feel about this place. At least, I thought I did from the way you talked.' He dragged the knot of his tie loose and unfastened his collar as if the crisp white shirt was choking him. 'Was that all it was? Just talk? No commitment?'

'Who are you to talk of commitment?' Kersty defied him, and the look in his eyes told her the shaft had gone home.

He crouched in front of her. 'It's different now. Look, I can't promise some other female won't creep out of the woodwork making extravagant claims about a past love affair. But I give you my solemn oath you will never, ever have to face anything like that alone. I will be right there beside you.' He gave a short, nervous laugh. 'How's that for a threat?'

Immediately serious again, he spoke with obvious effort, his voice low and desperate. 'Kersty, please, don't turn me down. I'd given up hope of ever finding a woman I could trust, someone who shared my ideals and understood what I'm trying to do. We make a perfect team, you and I.'

Didn't he know what he was asking of her? No, he didn't. For she had never told him that she loved him, that he was the other half of her. How could she work with him every day, watch all the plans for the estate come to fruition, share in the joys and sorrows, as a mere *colleague*?

'Neil, I——' Helplessly, she shook her head.

He stood up, his face bleak. 'It's the bloody title, isn't it?'

Her head jerked up and she gazed at him, bewildered. 'What is?'

'I thought you'd come to terms with it. Kersty, you must see I can't give it up. I haven't the right. It's a trust, to be passed on.'

Dazed, confused, her forehead puckered, 'What?'

'Is that why you won't marry me?' he demanded.

Her eyes flew wide. *'Marry you?'*

He glared at her. 'What the hell do you think I've been talking about for the past five minutes? Kersty?' He was on his knees in front of her. Taking the mug from her shaking hands, he set it on the tray. 'Kersty? Sweetheart?' His voice was raw with worry. 'Are you in pain again? Damn that bloody quack, the tablets should be working by now.' He tilted her chin, gently smoothing her hair back from her face. The concern scoring his face turned to perplexity, then to anger. 'Why are you laughing?' he demanded coldly.

Kersty felt light-headed. Relief, joy and overwhelming love, on top of all the recent harrowing events, were taking their toll.

'Oh, Neil, my dearest, dearest love, forgive me. I thought . . . I thought you were offering me a *business* deal.'

Enlightenment smoothed away the dark lines of strain. 'So I am,' he replied. 'An equal partnership. On one condition.'

'That I marry you?' How marvellous it was to say out loud words that had been merely a dream.

He nodded, cupping her head. 'I want to protect my investment.' His voice grew husky. 'Protect, support, honour and cherish.'

Kersty raised her hand to touch his face, drinking him in with eyes and fingertips. 'How I love you,' she whispered.

'I know,' he grated. 'I'll do my damnedest to be worthy of it—of you, Kersty.' He turned his face to kiss her palm.

'Kersty Drummond,' she sighed dreamily, a smile curving her lips.

'Viscountess Haldane,' he corrected, grinning as her eyes widened. 'It hadn't even occurred to you, had it?'

She shook her head, pulling a wry face.

'Do you think you can get used to it?'

She gazed at him. They had been through so much. They had both suffered. But they had emerged with a bond of love and trust that nothing and no one would ever break.

She smiled. 'I've got a lifetime in which to try.' And lifted her face to welcome his kiss.

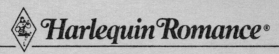

Harlequin Romance ®

Coming Next Month

2995 SOME ENCHANTED EVENING Jenny Arden
Eve has to admit that Zack Thole is persistent, and wickedly
handsome, but she is almost committed to Greg and has no
intention of being carried away by moonlight and madness. Yet
Zack can be very persuasive....

2996 LORD OF THE LODGE Miriam MacGregor
Lana comes to New Zealand's Kapiti coast to find the father she's
never known, having discovered he works at the Leisure Lodge
guest house. Owner Brent Tremaine, however, completely
misinterprets her interest in his employee. Surely he can't
be jealous?

2997 SHADES OF YESTERDAY Leigh Michaels
Necessity forces Courtney to approach old Nate Winslow for help.
After all, Nate owes her something—her mother had said so—
though Courtney doesn't know what. So it annoys her that his son
Jeff regards her as an undesirable scrounger!

2998 LOVE ON A STRING Celia Scott
Bryony not only designs and makes kites, she loves flying them—
and Knucklerock Field is just the right spot. When Hunter Green
declares his intention to turn it into a helicopter base, it's like a
declaration of war between them!

2999 THE HUNGRY HEART Margaret Way
Liane has steered clear of Julian Wilde since their divorce. But when
Jonathon, her small stepson, needs her help, she just can't stay
away—even though it means facing Julian again. After all, it isn't as
if he still loved her.

3000 THE LOST MOON FLOWER
Bethany Campbell

"Whitewater, I want you." These three desperate words not only
move lone hunter Aaron Whitewater to guide Josie through the
treacherous mountains of a tiny Hawaiian island to retrieve a
priceless stolen panda, they prove dangerously prophetic....

Available in August wherever paperback books are sold, or
through Harlequin Reader Service:

In the U.S.
901 Fuhrmann Blvd.
P.O. Box 1397
Buffalo, N.Y. 14240-1397

In Canada
P.O. Box 603
Fort Erie, Ontario
L2A 5X3

Have You Ever Wondered If You Could Write A Harlequin Novel?

Here's great news—Harlequin is offering a series of cassette tapes to help you do just that. Written by Harlequin editors, these tapes give practical advice on how to make your characters—and your story—come alive. There's a tape for each contemporary romance series Harlequin publishes.

Mail order only

All sales final
